WEASEL HUNT

WEASEL HUNT

A Novel of Suspense

James K. MacDougall

THE BOBBS-MERRILL COMPANY, INC.
Indianapolis / New York

Copyright © 1977 by James K. MacDougall

All rights reserved, including the right of reproduction in whole or in part in any form
Published by the Bobbs-Merrill Company, Inc.
Indianapolis   New York

Designed by Gail Conwell
Manufactured in the United States of America

First printing

Library of Congress Cataloging in Publication Data

MacDougall, James K.
    Weasel Hunt.

      I. Title.
PZ4.M1374We [PS3563.A2918]   813'.5'4   77-76881
ISBN 0-672-52337-X

To Carolyn

WEASEL HUNT

1

The snow started to fall as I drove to the office. At first a few flakes that might have been fly ash floated by; then the flakes became large enough that at the red light at Lake and West Boulevard I leaned over the steering wheel to look up at the sky. I sat back and looked over at the car stopped beside me in time to see that the driver had also leaned into his windshield. He turned and saw me. His mouth moved in an exaggerated manner—"It's snowing"—then he gave a shrug of despair. I smiled and shrugged back. We strangers shared, for a moment, helplessness over our immediate future.

The light changed and we separated. I drove down the ramp, through the underpass and up onto the shoreway. The traffic was heavy, as always, even late in the morning, but it moved rapidly at slightly over the speed limit. Before I was off at West 6th the snow fell in gusts, but not yet heavily. By the time I left the car in the parking garage and was up on the street, snow had begun to collect in the gutters and the cracks in the sidewalk, any place that sheltered it. I hurried into the protection of the building, across a dirty, wet terrazzo floor. Casually busy, the lobby seemed smaller today despite the stores that opened onto it.

When the elevator reached the fifth floor, Mary Farrar got on as I got off. She held the door button long enough to tell me hello, that I'd come back too soon, and that she'd drop by on her way back from the coffee shop. Mary ran a secretarial service on the same floor where I had my office. She'd been a Kelly Girl before she decided to open her own office. Between her good looks and her efficiency, and she made no bones about needing both, she'd made a success of it. She said she'd had enough of men with her first husband, but she knew what they liked and admired. Whenever I'd needed some work done she'd sent a girl over, and once in a pinch she'd done the job herself.

I opened the office and picked up the mail. I have two rooms—an unnecessary waiting room, since I work by myself and my work usually comes by referral, and my office. I went in, put the mail on the desk and opened the curtains. The city was even grayer through the windows, and the snow, large dry flakes now, swirled down to the pavement. If it continued at this rate, the evening rush hour would be little worse than usual. For mid-January it was better than we had a right to expect. The autumn had been long and damp, with rain turning occasionally into slush. Now that winter was here, the ground was hard, ready to hold the snow.

Most of the mail was uninteresting, ads and bills, a late Christmas card reminding me that now was the time to buy a new car from John "Bud" Selig. There were a couple of letters. The first, from a friend in Chicago, asked me if I were free to do some work with him. It was an industrial security case. I like Chicago and thought of the change as I opened the second. It was locally postmarked, and as I unfolded the letter two one-hundred-dollar bills fell out on the desk. The typed note was short and simple.

> Dear Mr. Stuart:
> The two hundred dollars enclosed is a retainer. At three o'clock January 16 go to 107 Green Hills Drive, the entrance to the Larch estate. You will know what to do when you get there.
> I will be in touch with you tomorrow at your office.

Today was the sixteenth; I looked at the bills. They were real, used; and the numbers not consecutive. I picked up the two letters and held them in opposite hands, literally weighing an action. I decided I could wait until later this afternoon to call Chicago.

I put the two letters side by side on my almost bare desk and put the two hundred dollars in an empty cash box, then turned the combination to lock it. The ads, along with Bud's, went into the wastebasket unopened before I started to open my bills. They were what I'd expected in a mixture of personal and business items, and I'd come in planning to pay them. The anonymous letter was too much to ignore, so I read it again. Still there was nothing special about it, other than its obviously enigmatic content. The phone book showed a B. H. Larch and a Benjamin Larch at that address. I got out a city map to check my memory that Green Hills Drive was a main north-south road through Green Hills, between Gates Mills and Hunting Valley, just inside the county line.

The outer office door opened. "Dave, you busy?"

It was Mary. She was in the office before I answered. Even in a tailored blue and gray houndstooth suit and little makeup she was trim and absolutely female. "Here, it's from the office, not that counter downstairs. Just a little milk. Right? Or have you changed your tastes in the last ten days?"

"No, they're still the same. Thanks."

She put the white styrofoam cup on my desk, looked at me for more information, then sat down in the brown vinyl chair opposite me. "You look good." She smiled approval. "Somebody should use you in an ad." I nodded a second thanks. "How was the weather?"

"Not bad. Rained a couple of days, but it was clear the rest of the time, so I could walk."

"You just walk?"

"Yes. Or read." I smiled. "I go to rest."

She nodded. "Many people?"

"No."

"Too isolated?"

"Not really; wrong season. Most tourists don't want sandbanks for the new year."

"Wrong time for those college kids. The one year I had in college we just went home. Now they all sound condemned if home is suggested." She took out a pack of cigarettes, the reason she had gone to the coffee shop, and I pushed an ashtray closer to her edge of the desk. "Maybe their parents would rather buy them off and send them to Florida or Bermuda."

"Not all that many, I hope. You're probably right, though." She shrugged and exhaled smoke. "What's made you so serious? You're supposed to be relaxed. You tired?" Then she noticed and swept her hand over the map, phone book and letters. "You working already?"

"Take a look at this." I handed her the anonymous letter.

"Where's the money?" she asked when she finished.

I gave a small laugh. "Is that the businesswoman or the woman asking, Mary?"

"That was just me. I know what it is to balance the books."

"I put it away until tomorrow."

"Are you going to go?"

"Yes."

"It could be a setup." Then her frown broke into a guileless smile. "Surely not everyone loves you the way I do."

"All too true. But it's more likely to be a joke. And you quit watching those TV detectives."

She tilted her head, then looked at the note again. "There's nothing here to help. Pica type, probably new or seldom used. Dime-store stationery and envelope. Only a name and address. Are they real?"

"Yes." I tapped the phone book.

"You called them?"

"There's no reason. They probably don't know anything about this. I'll have to wait till tomorrow for a straight answer — if I get one then. The best thing to do is go out and look around. Maybe I'll bump into the writer before tomorrow."

"You be careful, even if it is the middle of the afternoon."

"I love you, too." I blew her a kiss.

"Fresh. That's what happens when you go to a lonely beach by yourself."

"It'll be a joke."

"Expensive joke."

"Someone will want his money back."

"Don't we all." She crushed her cigarette and looked around. "Your office looks good, but you ought to do something to that waiting room. I like those drapes." Foxes, hounds, horses and men charged across the pleated wall behind me. "They're you—male, sexy."

"How many times you been in here?"

"Okay, so I could have said so before now. What's wrong with trying to cheer you up?"

"Nothing. Only I never think of them."

"Subliminally." She put her finger on her temple and nodded her head once at me; then stood up.

"I bet I'm the only detective you know who has sexy drapes."

"You're the only detective I know. But you do something about that waiting room or I'll be the only woman the office will seduce."

"The office, not me?"

"Try me. You got any work you want done?"

"Not today." I knew she was curious about why I'd gone away, but she would wait to ask.

"Okay. I've got to go. Not all of us get two hundred dollars in the morning mail. If someone wants his money back, you just ask what money."

I watched her go out and listened to the sound of her heels clicking steadily down the hall before the outer door closed. I found myself believing she couldn't have been so attractive at twenty as she was now. Maybe I thought so because I was closer to forty than to twenty.

I paid the bills, called the answering service—one call from Chicago included—and finally managed to kill enough time that I thought I could drive out. The snow was now falling only intermittently, so it seemed we would be spared winter's onslaught, something most people dread and simply want to get over, even when it means wishing away three or four months of their lives every year. Only skiers and children could mourn the passing of those days of gray sky and soot and snow-covered ground. I was as foolish as everyone else.

In every direction the city was built out farther and farther, as we tried to find safe new enclaves for pristine life—a search for Eden that revealed how foolish we were, for we'd lost paradise before we knew it. At least most of us had, but not a fortunate few, like those on Green Hills Drive. They or their ancestors had known what they were doing, leaving the rest of us to wonder if original sin applied to all. The fact that there were so few of them—a mailbox every few hundred yards, sometimes a half-mile—was not meant to encourage the rest of us. Maybe Eden and the American dream were still possible, though limited space would force us to take turns in paradise. All those tract houses by the freeway between shopping centers and factories, like so much litter scattered by passing conquistadors looking for El Dorado on Green Hills Drive, could only stand and rot, while their owners dreamed.

I took Interstate 90 to Mayfield. A couple of miles east and I was on Green Hills Drive, which rose and fell comfortably under me, not with the suddenness that reminds one of a roller coaster, but with the movement that varies perception, making each sight new. It was a pleasurable luxury, something that driving in the city was not. I was enjoying the light through the snow clouds as it caught the gray and brown bark, or the white of the fences that some had used to announce their success.

The Larches had put up a stone wall, as I eventually learned when I came to their mailbox and driveway. The entrance was a large turnaround at the top of a small rise, where the stone wall curved expansively back from the road and ended in a railed counterbalanced gate that was open. Two baby-blue police cars were in the turnaround. A bulky policeman who wore a dark blue nylon parka and carried a red signal flashlight waved me on, but I pulled in. He walked over in a rapid, clipped pace that his size stressed. Not angry but thinking hard about me, he was beefy enough to give the appearance of authority.

"I waved you on. You got business here?" His jaw shot out with what was meant to be a rhetorical question, so it dropped back when I said yes. Then he collected his thoughts, obviously in doubt. "You know the Larches?"

"No." He was more surprised this time, the tautness of his cheeks collapsed into round hemispheres that gave him an almost cherubic appearance despite his bulk. "Then what the hell do you want?"

I shut off the engine and got out. "Who's in charge here?"

"Lieutenant Carlson. But he's up at the house." He pointed through the open gates, obviously having forgotten his question.

"What's going on here?"

"I'm not sure, but it's serious. They're digging . . ." Then he looked at me again with suspicion. "What business you got here?"

"I think I should wait to tell your lieutenant."

His face didn't change, but he finally said, "You stay right here, then. Right here. I gotta go back to the road." He moved away, shifting his big, sulking shoulders from side to side emphatically. He looked back at me once, and I thought he wanted to say something, but he rubbed his left hand over his jaw and turned away.

The wall was about four feet high, but the ground on which it was built rose another four feet above the driveway where I stood. I couldn't see anything except the trees. Snow had blown against the wall, leaving the bank beneath it bare and brown-gray. Above a slight wind I could hear voices and a faint scraping sound. I pulled my overcoat collar up and walked toward the gate, beyond which the private drive slashed the trees.

Through the gray trunks and branches, I saw a group of men, all uniformed but one slight bald man, working under the boughs of a blue spruce that was thirty feet to the right of the gate just inside the wall, and their digging was the sound I had heard. Almost simultaneously there came two voices, one from the group—"Jesus, he was right!"—the other, the patrolman on the road—"Hey, you!"

The discovery under the tree must have been more important than my appearance, for as I walked in long strides toward the group no one looked at me or toward the sound of the voice behind me. I walked steadily, deliberately, the branches of small trees whipping past me, and I reached the spruce before my pursuer placed a hand on my shoulder. Then he too looked, as I did, into the hole, sheltered by the lower branches of the

7

spruce, where the bald man had stepped. He had pulled his dark gray overcoat up over his hips, so that it would not be soiled by the moist ground in the hole where he was brushing aside the dirt from the foot and calf of a human skeleton. It was ten minutes of three.

The man worked patiently up the calf to the knee, as though he were cleaning a burned area without injuring it. When he reached the knee he stopped, and stared at what he had uncovered. The ground over the torso was undisturbed. There were several shallow trenches beside the one that started about four feet below the skeleton's foot. He stood up, forgetting the tree limbs which scratched at his bare head, and then ducked as he climbed out of the hole. Two other patrolmen in identical nylon parkas peered over the handles of the shovels they held in front of them. Their faces were appropriately serious as they waited to hear what the detective would say.

I caught his eye and he turned on the man behind me. "God dammit, Bannister, get him out of here!" He thrust his arm back toward the gate.

"I told him he had to wait outside," Bannister pleaded.

"What the hell do you mean—wait? You weren't to let anyone stop."

"I told him I had to see whoever was in charge." The younger of the other two patrolmen snorted, then held his jaw tense. "Are you Carlson?" The man started to turn, but decided it was too late to make the effort.

"He's not back yet. I expect him at any time." He looked up the road, which disappeared over a small hill, then turned to the two men behind him. "Varner, you go with Bannister. Take this man with you, and make sure he doesn't leave. And call the coroner. Tell him we need his man. And call Lieutenant Carlson. He'll want to be here."

The three of us walked back to the road. I got in my car and turned on WCLV. A string quartet, modern and unfamiliar, drowned out the crackling of the police radio.

2

A Beethoven piano trio followed. I waited almost fifteen minutes, trying to find comfort in the music and in the English sparrows on a branch reaching out toward me over the wall. I couldn't hear them, but they were darting and bickering at one another. In cycles they dove into the brown trees, blending with them, and then returned to their perches.

The discovery of the skeleton would force me to show the police the letter and tell them my absurd story, what little there was to tell. I would be expected to supply opinions, if not answers. And I had no answers, only questions.

A few minutes after the sparrows disappeared into the woods, not to return, a dark green unmarked car came up the road from the house. The driver was alone. He parked the car in the drive at the gate and disappeared behind the wall. I caught a glimpse of a black raincoat. It was three-forty before he and the short, bald detective came through the gate. Bannister had been watching edgily, since the third car stopped, for their appearance. He made a friendly, sheepish wave with his flashlight. The short one made no sign, but the one who must have been Carlson nodded his head without taking his hands out of his coat pockets. Bannister was rebuked and turned back to the road. Carlson, too, was bareheaded, his coarse, sandy hair blowing in the breeze like the dried weeds by the wall. His hair was longer than most suburban cops'. He told the other detective something, then sent Varner back through the gate, came over and got into the passenger side of my car.

"It's colder than a witch's tit out there. Where's your ashtray?" He dug into his shirt pocket, pulling out a pack of Marlboros. I flipped open the ashtray and punched the lighter; I decided to say nothing. He used matches instead. He didn't want to owe me a light, not yet. He inhaled once.

"What's your name?" There was a band of freckles the color of his hair across his nose and underscoring both eyes.

"David Stuart."

"What'd you stop for?"

"I'm a private detective."

He pressed his lips against his teeth and made a sucking noise. "You're pretty fast." He turned off the radio.

"I was paid to be here."

"Let me see your license."

I had already reached my wallet and held it open for him. He didn't take it or ask me to remove the license.

"Put it away." He sucked on the cigarette. "What do you mean, you were paid?"

"I received this today." I took out the letter and gave it to him. "There was two hundred dollars, so I felt obligated."

"Commendable ethics." He snapped his cigarette at the ashtray and missed. The ash landed on my side of the drive shaft and rolled in one piece down the carpet. I pressed my right foot on it and waited. It was easy to see this would be a warm relationship.

"You've never been here before?"

I shook my head. "No."

"Then why do you think you were chosen?"

"I don't even know who chose me."

"How do you think we knew where to dig?" He made the move.

"Anonymous letter?"

"Phone calls. Three of them. All since eleven o'clock. A man, muffled his voice."

"He wanted to be sure you'd come."

"And before you got here." The first observation to connect

the two of us. "He even said he'd call the newspapers if we didn't look by three today." He drew hard on the cigarette. "I want to be there when you meet him tomorrow."

"Do you have all day?"

"I'll be there." He flicked his cigarette again. This time he hit the ashtray.

I waited for him to speak again. He didn't, so I ventured, "Did you learn anything at the house?"

"You'd think it was your case. If I decide to tell you something, I will. You gotta share with me; I decide what you get. You want to keep your license. So don't pull any crap on me tomorrow, cause I'll bust your ass fast."

All too true, and not intended to encourage trust.

"Sure. What can I say?" I shrugged in mock helplessness that Carlson missed. Okay. That was the way it would be. I preferred to work alone anyway. All I had to do was be sure he couldn't prove I withheld anything. "Would you mind if I went up to the house and made a few inquiries?"

He looked at me, the flat planes of his cheeks setting off small, soft brown eyes with almost no whites and pale lashes, like little animal eyes; then snorted. "Sure. You think you know so much, you go ahead. But you stop and see me on the way out."

"Can I have the letter?"

"It's evidence."

"I want to see if I get any reaction."

"Okay, but you damn well give it back on your way out." He acted as though he were gangbusters giving public enemy number one a subpoena as he shoved the letter against my hand. He started to get out. Mary wasn't the only one to watch too much TV.

"Lieutenant, would you mind moving your car?"

He slammed the door and shouted to the bald-headed man to move it for him. Carlson wasn't lovable, so I would avoid him. It was the best way to deal with a surly cop who could make good his threat to take my license.

Suburban murder makes headlines. Somebody killed in a tavern brawl or a tenement may make the front page, but not the headlines. But when a businessman kills his wife and her lover, it's a whole new world. The purity is broken, and the undercurrent that everyone knows is there becomes the flood. And as the illusion, the dream, is swept away, there is a dirty residue of excitement and tension. A compound of fear and gratification, depending on the level of society observing. Carlson knew the flood would break and he couldn't take comfort in the next few hours. He might be up most of the night, and the reporters would hound him. He would be pursued, while he had nothing to pursue. If he got quick results, he would be a hero. Otherwise, the goat. Still, I didn't feel for him.

His car pulled up beside me and I drove on back, leaving the police waiting for the coroner. Even in the leafless trees it came as a surprise, after pulling out of a sharp downward curve to the left, over a roll at the foot of a hill, then to the right and up a great open hill of browned grass, to see a rambling white-shingled house. The land opened with the suddenness of a well-lighted room on a wet, dark night. I had the feeling of driving a coach up to an eighteenth-century English inn. It was another world, cut off from the present by a woods and an eminence. Yet its solidity made it real. It belonged where it was. Since no one was at the door to change my horses, I came back to reality.

Unlike an inn, the house had a great silence about it—no cars, no movement. It might have been unused. I had purposely avoided asking Carlson who would be at the house, not wanting his judgment to interfere with what I saw, and he had seemed satisfied with the arrangement, not volunteering any information. A maid answered the door after my second knock and caught me surveying the view down the slope into the woods. A middle-aged woman with light brown skin, wearing a white uniform, she seemed out of place in the English scene that had slipped back into my mind as I gazed into the woods. She coughed in a manner that told me she was inclined to snap her fingers but would momentarily tolerate me.

"It's a lovely view." I motioned in a conciliatory effort. "My name is Stuart, and I'm here on the matter that brought Lieutenant Carlson."   She took a measure of me, doubtfully, before replying, "Wait inside the door, Mr. Stuart."

She stepped back far enough to allow me in, but she clearly intended that I stay by the door. "I'll be right back." She went down a hall into the back of the house.

The entryway was a large room with a wide stairway rising from the center toward the back wall and a three-sided balcony. But other than a secretary, two straight chairs, a large dropleaf table and some drab oil paintings, it was empty. Antiques, they were used and not museum pieces. On the table was a salver. Casting an eye around the balcony, I walked over to thumb through the mail the salver held. As could be expected, there was nothing resembling the letter I had received. The maid didn't return, but in a couple of minutes a man in his mid-thirties came out.

"Mr. Stuart, I'm Ben Larch." He extended his hand. "I understand you know something about the body." He had a steady, no-nonsense grip.

"I'm sorry if you got that impression. On the contrary, I hoped you could help me."

His face fell; then the forehead wrinkled in genuine curiosity. "Well, is there a body on our property? Lieutenant Carlson said one was reported, and they were going to dig near the road."

So the caller had told the police what to look for. He knew their needs and mine were different. "There is a body—a skeleton."

He shook his head and frowned. "But how would we know anything?" He gave a slight smile. "The police asked if they might dig. You really do know more than we do." He made a looping motion with his left hand. "By the way, are you with the police?"

"I'm a private investigator." Before he could respond I went on, "You said we."

"My mother, my wife and myself. I also have a younger brother, but he happens to be out now."

"Could I meet your wife and mother?"

He looked skeptical. "You've never even told me what your interest is." His voice was slightly firmed, but not unpleasant.

"If you wouldn't mind, I would like to tell everyone."

"My mother is sixty, Mr. Stuart, and I would prefer to decide what she can safely hear on this unpleasant matter."

I took the envelope from my inside coat pocket and gave it to him. He read the address before looking at the contents. As he read the letter his face remained unmoved, and he replaced it in the envelope before returning it to me.

"Have the police seen that?" He pointed toward the envelope.

"Yes."

"And they let you keep it?"

"Temporarily." I smiled at his quickness.

"To show to me?"

"Apparently, though I wasn't told who was here."

"You are pretty obvious."

"Perhaps." I shrugged, for I was unsurprised by his condescension. "There's no reason not to be."

"No, of course not. I'll introduce you to my mother." He was unsure of me, yet determined to prove his family's ignorance of my letter. I told myself that were I in his situation I would do the same, whether I wanted to or had to.

He took my coat and hung it in the closet, then walked ahead of me in the direction the maid had taken. In the hall were some dark landscapes whose value was lost to me. The frames were impressive. We went through a double door on the left into an enormous drawing room–library. It was about forty feet long and twenty-five wide. Three walls were filled to the extraordinarily high ceiling with books. A ladder providing access to the upper shelves leaned in its track on the far wall. A fourth wall of small square-paned casement windows looked out onto a steep slope that was tree-covered and, judging from the level of the treetops, dropped off sharply. In the center of that wall three lemon velvet couches formed a square with the windows.

When we entered the room, two women were sitting in the corner closest to us, leaning toward each other over a small, fragile table, as though sharing a secret. Neither appeared to notice us, nor did they hasten to separate when the younger woman saw us. Larch walked over to stand behind his mother, without appearing to look at either, and introduced us.

In spite of her white hair, his mother did not appear to be sixty. Square shouldered, in a tan and yellow plaid suit, she looked as though she had only now returned from a charity board meeting, just as her daughter-in-law in a plain red jumper and lace-trimmed white silk blouse had come in from Junior League. The younger woman wore one piece of jewelry, a plain gold pin a couple of inches above her left breast; the other, none.

Larch hadn't mentioned the letter, apparently having decided to allow me the opportunity to test his family, so his mother asked immediately, "What could a private detective want with us, Mr. Stuart?" The voice was courteous but distant.

I gave her the letter without saying anything.

"Very strange. Read this, Leslie."

Larch's wife took the letter and after reading it extended the paper to me as if it were an account that she was unconcerned with, her lower lip crossing the upper for a second as she dipped her head toward her left shoulder, her auburn hair passing quickly over the white blouse and gold pin. She was about thirty, a few years younger than her husband.

"Did you think someone here sent it?" It was the mother.

"No, but I thought I should ask."

"The police thought he should, too," her son put in.

"I thought that policeman understood we were not to be disturbed." Her voice wasn't angry, but calm. She was used to having her way. "I hope I don't need to talk to his superiors."

"I don't think you'll need to. I requested that the lieutenant let me in. He knew nothing of the letter when he was here."

"He knew how I felt."

"That's a beautiful view across the valley." I wanted to relax the moment, and didn't want to leave yet. "Do the trees block it in the summer?"

"Not entirely. But the hillside is like a jungle. I don't know why Ben and Leslie wanted to build at the bottom of the hill." She accepted the change of subject, but not me.

"Not the bottom, but almost." Leslie was smiling at us, but without evident pleasure.

"Won't you sit down, Mr. Stuart? Would you like a drink?" asked Larch. As though to affirm his apparent desire to relieve any tension, he unbuttoned the coat of his plain blue suit. I returned the gesture by taking a light Scotch I didn't really want. He had the same, but didn't offer either his wife or mother a drink. I wondered if they didn't drink or whether we were chiefs sharing a peace pipe.

"Someone wants to hire you to investigate that body that was reported," said Mrs. Larch, returning to the immediate without condescension.

"It's a skeleton, Mother. Mr. Stuart saw it." He sat down beside his wife; I sat opposite his mother, remaining the outsider to their group.

"Will they be able to identify the body?" She seemed genuinely curious.

"Possibly from teeth or anything that might be buried with it."

"Oh, rather an unpleasant business, isn't it?"

"I think I'll go down to the house, dear." Leslie Larch patted her husband's knee and stood up. She was around the couch before I made a motion to stand. "It was nice to meet you, Mr. Stuart. Don't forget we are to go out tonight, Ben."

"No, I remember."

She seemed very formal, but she was a very attractive woman. It was hard not to watch her leave the room, though of the three of us remaining I seemed to be the only one with the problem. I looked after her again as I heard the click of the latch. Too late. The mother and son looked from each other to me.

Mrs. Larch spoke. "Leslie's a sensitive, intelligent girl." She spoke with finality, but her son echoed her opinion.

"Sensitive . . . or tactful?" I asked.

"Both." There was the same tone, but now it was not final. "But this time I should think it was sensitivity. I'm getting to be an old woman, and I hardly find the subject of skeletons appealing."

"Few people would, Mother."

"I only meant that someone as young as Leslie could hardly find the subject pleasurable."

Perhaps they were right, too, that she did not want to hear.

"You don't recognize the type in that note?"

"No. But I can assure you that it is not from my typewriter, and it's the only one we have," Ben Larch said. His voice was cool, superior.

"I didn't mean to offend. But since the body was here, I couldn't help wishing for an easy lead."

"Of course, Mr. Stuart." Mrs. Larch now had the same innocuous tone her daughter-in-law had used before leaving the room. It seemed they might have been mother and daughter. "But as the policeman indicated, they are digging near the road. Much closer to the public than to us."

I took a swallow of Scotch as she finished and nodded. The silence was critical. So I decided to have another go at some questions, before it became any more obvious that I should leave.

"Would you mind if I asked a couple more questions? I have to tell you that I'm as puzzled as you. Someone, whoever wrote that note, paid me a retainer, and I should assume they wanted me, but why is a mystery."

"Why not?" Larch responded so quickly I almost laughed at the pseudo-philosophical form of our conversation. I found myself being as formal with them as they with me. "You must be in the phone book. You were probably chosen at random."

"Probably. Anyway, that's my problem." I tried to smile innocently. "I wondered if you knew of anyone around here who disappeared in the last couple of years—a servant, a neighbor."

"No. Our gardener quit last June—a very awkward time—but no one has disappeared. Besides, Mr. Stuart," Mrs. Larch went on, "would a murderer leave a body in the same neighborhood? That isn't very precise, I mean near where someone had disappeared." Precise was what she wished to be; she had described herself accurately.

"Possibly not, though carrying a body around isn't safe."

"Or comforting."

"No. And this situation is special, because someone now wants the body found."

"That seems the greatest puzzle," said Ben Larch. "Why, if he has been successful at hiding the body, would anyone wish to be known?"

"Yes, I think that's exactly the point." I saw that he was perfectly serious. "Only, don't you mean why would anyone want the body found? Finding who put it there is another step."

"Of course. That is what I meant. Anyway, perhaps you'll learn why tomorrow. If the person who sent that letter keeps his word."

"I'm not so sure I want to have anything to do with the case." I stood up, leaving my unfinished drink on the table. "Thank you for your time. I'm sorry to have intruded with something so unpleasant."

"We understand, don't we, Ben?" We were all standing, and she had gone over to her son and put her hand through his right arm. "You and the police must do your jobs." Her ice had thawed by will.

"Thank you for that. You have a beautiful house. Driving up from the front, I had been transported to an eighteenth-century estate."

"You're very perceptive, Mr. Stuart. Ben's father, my late husband, felt the same way. That's why we stayed in the house. He had quite a fine collection of eighteenth-century first editions." She extended her hand to the wall behind me, not pointing, only explaining, but I turned to look briefly. "Mostly British—he was a true Anglophile—but a few American. Do you have the same interest?"

"Not to that extent." I meant the wall filled with books. "But I find the past fascinating."

"Yes, it is." She was ready to talk further, but her son looked at his watch.

"Mother, you remember I have to go out this evening."

"Of course; I'm not that forgetful. Leslie said so when she left here." There was a coolness in her voice as well as her words. "I have some work to do, too." She took her hand from his arm, then walked over and extended it to me. "Perhaps you would be interested in seeing Ben's collection someday. It really is a fine one."

"That would be a pleasure." It would be, but I felt I spoke from politeness, as she had—that we were not likely to meet again. She had no reason to send me an invitation, or even offer a tentative one.

"I'll go out with you, Mr. Stuart." He turned to his mother, who now looked out the window, her head turned from us as she appeared to gaze at the valley and the two gray hills visible in a rapidly darkening day. It might snow yet. "If we're not late, I'll stop in to see you, Mother."

She turned around, a smile fixed on her face. "That would be fine. Good afternoon, Mr. Stuart." She was changeable, using, as many people do, affection and scorn to hold on to what she had.

Larch closed the doors behind us. Before he did, I saw Mrs. Larch turn on a light and go over to her husband's collection.

"Your father must have put a great effort into his book collection."

"Yes. It's all rather vague to me." Then, as though his feelings might sound too cool, "I mean his practices as a collector. I was only a child then. He died in an automobile accident when I was ten. Only when I was in college did I come to appreciate the value of what he was doing. The aesthetic and historical value, not the monetary." He added the last rapidly, as though I would misunderstand his motives. But there was no need to think otherwise. The Larches did not need to think of money.

He got our coats from the closet and, as I had said nothing, went on, "I suppose the whole family is made up of collectors. I deal in art objects and antiques. Even Leslie raises dogs—collies. She's very good with them."

"What about your mother?" I was buttoning my topcoat.

"She encourages us and keeps my father's collection in order." He made a smile. "She's made it possible for us to do as we please." I wondered if he included his father. "And I suppose it would be fair to say she collects people. Not in any Hollywood sense, not selfishly. Merely by chance and interest. She has a wide variety of interests. Serves is a fairer word than collects." He seemed satisfied with his explanation, and there was no reason to ask more. On the way to my car I asked where his gallery was—an address on Euclid—but I was simply being polite.

By the time I looked after him, he had disappeared around the driveway to the garages, and I supposed he had gone on down the hill to his own house. I drove slowly away from the house, paying as much attention to my rear view mirror as to the road. At the bottom of the slope I stopped to look back up. Even in the dusk, it was an eighteenth-century house, and I felt I had stepped right out of the past back to the present. The rest of the way back to the road I drove slowly. It was almost three-quarters of a mile from the house to the police cars at the gate. Rather than ask them to move again I took the opportunity to get out and walk over to the grave where the men were at work by lights.

Carlson saw me and came over to stop me. "Okay, Stuart, what did you learn?" His voice was unpleasant. He wanted to lean on me.

"Very little. The mother, son and daughter-in-law were there. The late husband collected rare books, and the son owns an art gallery."

He smiled. Obviously we had gotten the same information.

"How's the digging going?"

"Let me have the letter."

I gave it to him and repeated my question.

"Okay."

"Is there any identification?"

"It's not your case."

"I realize that, but I'm trying to cooperate."

"You have to. I don't. You can read about it like anyone else—in the papers. And don't forget to leave your office door open tomorrow. I'll be there early." He looked over my shoulder to a patrolman, shouting at him to move the car.

Back on the shoreway, I managed to get snarled in the rush-hour traffic over the bridge. I wasn't in any better humor for that. There had been no point in returning to the office. By the time I was home, I was angry as hell with Carlson and found myself hoping my anonymous correspondent would call or knock at the door. But through one Scotch nothing happened to change my mood, so I decided to cook dinner. I got out a sirloin, boned and trimmed it viciously, and carelessly. After dumping some peppercorns into a cheesecloth, I wrapped them and smashed them hard with a wooden mallet. I rubbed the skillet with a piece of fat and turned the heat up. By the time I had pressed the crushed pepper into the steak, the skillet was smoking angrily. I fixed another Scotch to have with the steak. While I was eating, I discovered that I had pushed several pieces of cracked pepper well into the meat.

3

It was a bad day for news. No presidential trips, no fights between the mayor and city council, no political kidnappings. So, *The Plain Dealer* headlined the story. The paper might have, anyway—the skeleton was headless. There was no identification—apparently the body had been buried nude—and no report on a preliminary examination beyond the fact that it was the skeleton of a man about six feet tall. Nor was there any mention of the letter, only the persistent calls to the police. But then I hadn't expected Carlson to alarm my correspondent. He wasn't even quoted as having a lead. A short column of information, when compared to the headline, with no further additions to what I knew. Whoever wanted the body found probably didn't want it identified.

I was wrong about my correspondent. No sooner had I put a coffee cup in the sink and the toaster back on the shelf than the phone rang. A pause followed my hello, so with some irritation I repeated myself and gave my name. This time a young man's voice replied.

"Mr. Stuart, you received my letter?"

"Yes. I was getting ready to go to the office."

"Could we meet someplace else?" The tentative voice surprised me.

"Yes. Where?" Fighting my whetted curiosity, I tried to sound as though we were negotiating the price of a pound of bologna.

He paused, then his voice was not so high-pitched; it relaxed slightly the next time he spoke. "At Forest Hills Park. Go out Mayfield and turn north on Monticello to Lee to the first parking lot."

"Now?"

He had already hung up, very probably afraid. I looked down at the front page and wondered if he knew the body was headless when he wrote me. Or if he were simply alarmed by the publicity. Whatever made him call me at home, I was pleased. No Carlson for now—I had at least a temporary advantage. I put on a tie and headed for the elevator. None of my neighbors was about.

There was a solitary beruffled grackle on the driveway as I pulled out of the apartment garage. He looked at me, mildly defiant—as he must have been to remain so late in the winter—then flew into some bushes that quivered from the wind off the lake. The sky was a plain, flat gray. The threat of snow apparently had passed. Perhaps the day would clear. The grackle was the most interesting thing I saw on my drive. The morning traffic moved with its commonplace sporadic action, punctuated only by the occasional maniac who raced from stoplight to stoplight and lane to lane. There were days when I tired of city life.

When I pulled into the parking lot, mine was the only car present. I let the engine run. The trees about the lot had a few leaves, but nothing living, man or animal, stirred. I looked back to the street, but the only cars there were moving. Then I saw him moving toward me across a field. I sat, waiting for him to become distinct. The dark coat became a green wool parka with an upturned hood. He was young and wary, his pace slowing almost imperceptibly when he was close enough to focus on me through my windshield. His brown hair fell over his forehead and from the right side of his hood. His face was red with cold. He might have been walking for some time. When he stopped next to me, I rolled down the window and caught the same cold air across my face.

"Mr. Stuart?"

It was the voice on the phone.

"Get in." I rolled up the window and unlocked the passenger

door. He brought the cold in with him. It hung from his clothes, as the fear had from his voice.

"Do you have my letter? For identification."

"The police do." He was startled. "You should know they would after yesterday."

His eyes, pale blue, almost as pale as ice, contrasted with his face, almost as though they were holes. So far, the fear of his voice and eyes was the only emotion he had shown. I showed him some identification. He looked at it closely, but blankly, so that I couldn't be sure he was reading. When he closed my wallet to return it, he sank down in his seat with a shiver. He was about twenty, and from his face I could see only that he was tired and nervous.

"Want to tell me who you are and what this is about?"

He nodded and sighed. "Here, read this." He took an envelope from his right coat pocket and handed it to me. On the outside was typed: FOR ROBERT STEDMAN.

"Is this your name?"

"Yes."

The paper was ordinary white tablet notepaper; the envelope was equally undistinguished. Available in any drugstore. The typed contents were not.

December 1967

Dear Robert,

By the time you receive this note I shall have long since disappeared from your life. Perhaps that is for the best. Do not blame your mother for anything. Try not to blame me. But if you feel any anger or hurt, I am responsible.

When you read this you will be a man, and so I feel I can leave you with a request. Ask the police to dig on the east side of the blue spruce south of the driveway, near the main road. I would not involve you if there were anyone else I could trust.

Love,
Father

I tried to take in all the possibilities of the letter and not to ask about too many. It was best to allow Stedman some room. I saw that he ignored me as I read, but he could not be as indifferent as he seemed.

"Your name is Stedman, but the body was on the Larch property."

"Marian Larch is my mother."

"Your father . . . ?"

"Her second husband." He was not looking at me, but through the windshield. His breathing was now barely audible.

"You called the police?"

"Yes."

"Why did you hire me? You must have known the police would handle the matter, no matter what they found. Or did you know they were being asked to open a grave?" I kept watching him, but he didn't turn to look at me, and I couldn't be certain he was holding back.

"No. I had no idea. Or rather I had guessed. But it was a wild guess." So he used it to entice the police to act.

"What had you guessed?" I felt as though I were leading a small child, though it crossed my mind that I may have been the one being led. Nevertheless he had opened up some. He had to have a great deal on his mind.

"That he might be dead. That 'long since disappeared' was a euphemism for dead."

I nodded, then asked, "Has the thought that he might have put that body there crossed your mind?"

He looked at me for the first time. His face was flushed. Only a few minutes before, he had exuded cold; now spots of perspiration stood on his upper lip and just beneath his hairline. "Yes . . . yes. Would you turn down the heat?" Then he looked away.

"Shall we drive for a while?"

He shrugged, so I backed from the parking space, drove around the lot and back onto Lee Road. I let him sit, hoping he would say more. We crossed Euclid and came to 152nd Street. He failed to respond to the opportunity. I headed for the shoreway again, thinking he might relax with open road ahead of him, and my not staring at him. Moreover, he would not be able to run if we were doing fifty. He was edgy enough for anything.

"Would you mind telling me why your mother changed her name, and what happened to your father?"

"No, not at all. I'm surprised you heard nothing when you went to the house yesterday." In the next forty-five minutes we talked intermittently, and he eased himself by telling me the basic facts behind the letter.

"What did they say about my visit?"

"Leslie told me about the policemen and you. But she said she hadn't listened to what was said."

"She didn't. Not to what I said, at least. You like her?"

"Yes." He paused as though to add something but stopped.

"You were going to tell me why your mother changed her name."

"My mother has strong feelings and a strong will. She really hates my father. Strange, isn't it, that I should side with him, when he hasn't been around for ten years? Isn't a son supposed to love his mother and hate his father? Especially in my situation?" He laughed, a sharp, false laugh. I kept my eyes on the road, intent on letting him talk, but from the corner of my eye I saw him take a key ring from his pocket and spin it around in his hand.

We pulled onto the parallel entrance road at 152nd Street and soon were racing east in heavy traffic. A white Cadillac came into the rear view mirror and was on my tail immediately. It cut to the right and squeezed back in front of us, maneuvering between my right front fender and a semi. No sooner did he get by us than he cut to the left around the next car and floored it. I was more irritated than usual by such driving. We were going the same way I had gone the day before, but this time I didn't cut off at the Outer Belt. I noticed that Stedman looked up as we went on east.

"My father deserted my mother ten years ago. For another woman. He's barely a memory now. My mother burned all the pictures we had of him . . . except for this snapshot." He put the keys back in his pocket and pulled a black and white picture from his right pocket. "Here, you may need this."

I took the picture, holding it in my right hand at the top of the steering wheel. It was of a man and a boy on a pier, their fishing rods erect beside them, but no fish showing. The boy, about ten, was a small version of the young man sitting beside me. He was in jeans, with a striped pullover knit shirt. The man was about forty, dark haired and of average height. He had on chinos and an alligator shirt. The picture was overexposed in a bright sun, but they made a handsome pair who might have come out of a toothpaste ad or a cereal commercial.

"How did you save this?" I put it in my inside coat pocket.

"It was in a book, a Hardy Boys adventure. I came across it several years ago and saved it. When I received the letter, I took it out."

"What was your father's name?"

"Paul Stedman."

"When did your mother divorce him?"

"As soon as she could. A year after he left. Then she took her first husband's name."

"Was your father younger than your mother?"

"How did you know?"

"It's not difficult to see that he was about forty when that picture was taken, and I met your mother yesterday."

"There's seven years' difference between them. I don't know if that contributed to the separation. It might have, but it's just as possible that money came between them."

"Whose?"

"My mother's, of course." The point was obvious for him.

"Are you their only child?"

"Yes. Ben is Mother's by her earlier marriage."

He had become relaxed. The more he talked, the more the knots disappeared from his thoughts and his voice. The traffic had thinned out. I kept going between fifty-five and sixty. I decided to try something harder on him.

"You want me to find your father, no matter what?"

"Yes. Even if that's his skeleton. I want to know."

"Even if he killed the person in the grave?"

"Yes." The answer was quick enough to indicate that the thought was not new.

"Okay, I'll work for you. Let's head back." I pulled off at the next turnoff, then headed back west.

We still had to talk over some points, but I wasn't worried about him for now.

"Did the letter seem strange to you, Mr. Stedman?"

"Bob. The typing? Yes. It could have been sent by anyone was what occurred to me after I got over the shock. That, and the fact that it is so impersonal." His second observation again revealed some thought. He wasn't living with any illusions, which helped.

"Right. Of course it's possible that in ten years you were to feel nothing, so the letter was to show nothing. How did you come by the letter?"

"The family lawyer, Alec Bolen, called me two weeks ago. He gave it to me on my twenty-first birthday, just as a letter of instructions had directed him."

I suddenly felt sorry for Bob. It was a lousy way to come of age. But his voice revealed no self-pity, and I said nothing.

"He received it ten years ago?" The exits were now choked with motels, offices, trailer parks and neon. More and more houses were visible. I'd decided to drive back to the Forest Hills Park, unless he asked me to stop.

"Yes. I asked him."

"What about the other woman you mentioned?"

"Ellen Penn. She was the wife of my father's partner."

"Where can I find him?"

"In Lakeview Cemetery. He died about two months after his wife left him"—his voice was neutral, without pity or contempt—"in a plane crash in Chicago."

"Does anyone know what happened to them—your father and Mrs. Penn?"

"If they did, no one ever said anything to me."

"No missing persons reports?"

"I don't know. I remember I was told my father had gone away on business. And a little later that he had died. But that was all. That and the burning of the pictures."

"And life went on as usual?"

"I was only eleven. I didn't know about the divorce until I

started asking about my mother's new name. Then I was told what happened."

"Earlier you said your mother hates your father." There were many more cars now that we were near the city, but we kept going at just over fifty.

"She does. We never talk of him. But I slipped up—just before my birthday. Actually, I was hurt." He smiled ruefully. "He *is* my father, and it's been hard never even mentioning him. It's surprising how hard it is not to talk of a father." He paused slightly. "You know, it just occurred to me how hard it must have been for her not to talk of someone she hated so. She's not a bad person. And he doesn't seem terrible in my memory—or maybe it's just that picture I gave you—sentimental, isn't it?"

"Maybe—feelings are blurred after years. I know my childhood must seem better than it actually was." I smiled at him. "Isn't everyone's better or worse with years?"

"What do you think your chances of finding him are?" His voice was earnest, and probably hopeful.

"That depends on whether the past is completely cold. I'll have to do some checking. We might as well start with your family." I turned off at 185th Street and drove through Euclid Creek Reservation to Green Road. "Can you face an open discussion?"

"Yes. I knew I would have to when I hired you. You'll need to know as much as possible, and I'm not much help."

You're a big boy now, I thought. I found I liked him—I wanted to find his father for him. I told myself to slow down—that it was likely that everything was cold.

"Set up an appointment this afternoon. Do what you think is best to have your family there, even if you don't tell them about me. I'm going back to my office. I'll give you the number. If I'm out, simply tell the answering service the time. I'll make any apologies for the meeting. By the way, you haven't shown anyone else the letter?" We were back in the parking lot.

"Of course not."

"I'll keep it. Unless you object."

"No. Will you show it to the police?"

"Not for now. I should, but I'm not going to. Nor am I going to say who called them yesterday. Until we know how your father and that body are connected, I think we should wait." I encouraged my feelings about Carlson to stand in the way, but I told myself the evidence was shaky.

"Anyway, can you arrange to have your family at home?"

"I'll try. Ben may be out. Should I wait if he is?"

"Yes. We should be there together. What kind of partnership was your father in?"

"Some stores of some kind. You'll have to ask someone else."

We pulled into the parking lot and I took a card from my wallet. "That will get you an answering service, but they'll put you through. Don't waste time on reaching me." I looked at my watch—ten-thirty. Still time enough to meet them.

"Thank you for helping me." He extended his right hand and smiled for the first time.

"Thank me when I've done something. I'll expect to hear from you."

"You will, by noon." He got out of the car and walked back the way he had come across the brown grass. The day remained dingy. Even the wind could not clear the sky. I waited until he was almost out of sight and then started for the office.

The case now had too many possibilities. Only one fact remained clear: Stedman's father knew about the body. Or was it a fact? Was it his body, discovered because of a note someone had written ten years earlier after murdering him? No, there were no facts. No identity to the note or the skeleton.

I drove down Chester. Near 81st Street several black children darted between cars to cross the street. The buildings looked bombed out, and the children could be taken for refugees from an invading army. But this wasn't land anyone invaded. We had all retreated to whatever comfort and quiet we could find.

4

Mary's office door was open; several typewriters were snapping at one another. I went down to say good morning and to use her Xerox copier. Mary was in her cubicle, a glass enclosure on the outside wall of a large room. Several girls were working at the typewriters. All were attractive, in keeping with Mary's view that man wanted an attractive secretary as much as, maybe more than, an efficient one. But she wouldn't slack on the latter either. They all said hello, as I did, even though I knew only a couple by name. I was glad I'd come down, because I needed to see something beautiful.

Mary was on the phone, her back to the room, when I came in, and her right arm moving in the air. When she turned around she saw me and waved me to a chair. She finished arguing a minimum time for a job, to her satisfaction, and hung up. I sat opposite her.

"Jesus, that cheap son of a gun. But I got him." She lighted a cigarette with a large square teakwood lighter, the only extra in the room, a gift from me. "I'm glad you came in, Dave. There's been a cop here looking for you."

"I expected that. Was he mad?"

She inhaled as she nodded her head. "Pounded on your door. That's why we heard him. Said he'd be back before noon."

That didn't leave much time if Carlson was true to his word, as I expected him to be. I had Mary make a copy of the letter. Then I went down the street to my bank to put the original in my deposit box. It was almost twelve when I left the bank, so I found a pay phone and reached Steve Horning in the prosecutor's office. He gave me a quick rundown on Carlson.

"He's a tough cop, Dave, physically tough. Bad business. Police brutality is a phony charge a lot of the time, but not with Carlson. The reports came in too often, and one stuck. He was lucky to avoid prosecution."

"How'd he keep his badge?"

"He couldn't in the city."

"And the prosecution?"

"A couple of buddies perjured themselves. At least we're pretty sure."

"How'd he get his job in Green Hills?"

"Can't be sure. Had a good record of arrests in vice—that can be hell on a man, too. And he had some good references, connections. It's just as likely that the brutality charge got him the job."

I laughed. "You mean an edgy suburb."

"Sure. A tough cop gets a lot of respect in suburbia. Keeps life clean for them. No criminal element."

"While you pick up after the scum." I was sympathetic.

"That's about it." He sounded resigned, the careful modulation gone. Then he repeated himself with even greater heaviness that was easy to read, "Yeah, that's it."

"Has he had any trouble on his new job?"

"Not until yesterday." He laughed. "He should have a good time with that potato. Son of a bitch, it couldn't have happened to a nicer guy." He laughed longer. I decided he must be having a bad day. "That's a suburb of paranoid little old ladies. Every time some Jew grocer in Hough gets shot, they figure the revolution is here. There are two private patrol services out there and enough guns . . . oh, what the hell!" He paused; I could hear his breath. "Is there anything else, Dave?"

"Not today, thanks." I was grateful for the answers, but especially for not being asked why. Steve had enough sense not to ask me to lie to him, and so he didn't ask questions. He never did, and I always tried to repay a favor.

Carlson was by my office door when I got back. Mary must have told him to wait. His raincoat was open, he looked warm, and he held his narrow-brimmed hat in his left hand. He jerked it, holding the brim, so it rotated. He watched me come down the hall, but remained against the door jamb.

"You keep better hours than a banker." He moved grudgingly.

"Sometimes. I can't complain about the advantage of being my own boss."

I put the key in the door and went in ahead of him. There was no mail. I took off my coat, hung it in the small closet off the inner office, and sat down behind the desk, waiting for him to ask me about the letter. He had thrown his coat over a chair and was already seated.

"I presume you heard from your client?"

"Not yet."

"Then where have you been all morning?"

"On some errands. I'm not married, so I have to take care of the dry cleaning myself."

He shifted his weight around, putting his right leg over his left knee. "Cut that crap, Stuart. You really expect me to believe that?"

"You should, but I can't help what you believe." I leaned on the desk, my left hand on my temple. "I sympathize with you. It's not an easy case. And headlines like this morning's only draw attention."

"I don't want your sympathy. I want to know who sent you that letter."

"I can't tell you what I don't know. I learned only from this morning's *PD* that the skeleton was headless. Why, you didn't even tell them how the victim died."

"We don't tell more than we know, either. There were no marks on the skeleton."

"You mean he'd never had a broken bone?"

"Not on what we have now."

"So you don't know how he died?"

"Cutting off the head is a pretty effective means to murder." He chuckled to himself. I smiled politely. Then he became serious. "Now I've told you what you want to know, haven't I?"

"You've told me what you want me to know. Or what I could have found out from the coroner's office."

He scowled. "Like hell you could. You want me to go after your license?"

That did it for me. But I didn't lose control. "It would be easier than finding the murderer."

"If I prove you've withheld evidence, it won't be hard to do."

"Go on. But I assure you that it will be harder than protecting rich industrialists and little old ladies."

"Okay, Stuart, I want to know where you were this morning. You smartass like that once more and . . . "

"What'll you do, work me over? You better face up to your problem—murder. I gave you the letter yesterday . . . now lay off."

I realized that I was too angry. The whole thing had started as a verbal game for me, but now I really disliked Carlson. With what Steve had told me I even hated him. I swiveled about in my chair and walked to the window and an increasingly dreary day. My anger was intense enough that I distrusted myself. Sure he was brutal and bad at his work, but what I felt was too strong for righteous anger. Then the little old ladies crossed my mind—Mrs. Larch. What Bob Stedman had told me made me realize how she had held back yesterday. I had not asked; she had not volunteered. Better to lose my temper now, I decided, because this afternoon she wouldn't be very happy to see me.

So I made up a couple of errands that he could never check—grocery and drugstore—and told him he would hear from me if I ever received a call. He bitched some more, but left, knowing I wouldn't call him.

To rid myself of Carlson's visit I took Mary to lunch. She asked a couple of discreet questions about my visitor and let me know that Carlson and I could be heard in the hall, but then dropped the subject. She told me about the musical in town that she'd seen a couple of nights before, and we talked about travel.

Right after our waitress put a fruit salad in front of her, Mary asked about Chris.

5

Chris was one of the reasons I had decided to go to Cape Hatteras after Christmas. Much of my childhood had been spent walking alone. Then I had been able to go out on a bicycle to find a field or hill; but those places were gone, bulldozed and cemented over into giant mausoleums. The need to be alone hadn't died, but now it was harder to release. In our brick-to-brick living we think adults who want solitude are eccentric; children, disturbed. So I must be mad, because I had driven seven hundred miles to be alone, to walk a wide beach under a puffy gray sky, in a cold wind, and to think about Chris and myself.

She is the only talented person I have ever known. She once told me I was the only independent person she had ever known. In the late summer and fall I think we each considered for the first time that we might be mistaken, and with that came the puzzle: what to think now, and what difference a mistake in judgment would make to the other and to ourselves. I never doubted my belief in her talent the way I did her belief in my independence. For one thing, talent is measurable or identifiable; independence is not. For another, I knew some of the reasons for my independence and questioned others. Chris played the violin—not just well but brilliantly. She had studied at the Institute and in New York, had placed in the Leventritt, and had come back to teach and study and to play second violin in a quartet that made a college circuit each year.

They had gone on a midwestern tour in early November and Chris had wanted me to come. We had stopped seeing each other in September, six or seven weeks earlier, when she called and invited me. She was, at once, resonant and lyric on the phone.

"But, Dave, you would enjoy it. And the others won't mind. Joan was asking about you last week. They'd be glad to see you. Howard and she won't object. You know them well enough to know that. And I want to see you, too. I've missed you."

"Have you?" My tone was doubtful, even cold, though I hadn't intended it to be. And she caught it.

"Of course I have." She wasn't hurt, simply direct. She meant what she said.

"I didn't mean that. I've thought of you, too. How have you been?"

"Busy. But don't change the subject and don't be so distant." She was right, on both counts. For a second I felt a panic: was I basically distant? I had thought before that perhaps I was because I admired her as much as I loved her, even when I failed to call her. She kept her voice playful when she corrected me with a patience I didn't deserve. Then she again said, almost sadly, "I've missed you."

I let the silence hang on her words and voice until they disappeared in me. Then I asked, "Can I see you tonight?"

"Yes."

"When would you like me to meet you?"

"Right now. I have another pupil waiting for me, but I can be free by two-thirty. I'll meet you by 'The Thinker.' Can you find me?"

"That's what I work at."

We hung up. For the next hour and a half I found myself unable to think of anything else. Then I saw her. She was waiting for me; she had to have cut the last student short. She put her hand in mine and into my overcoat pocket.

"Let's walk around the lagoon." So we walked down the steps as though nothing had changed. She hadn't. Her dark brown, almost black hair was still at neck length and brushed back from her face. The walk in the wind only made her eyes moist and darker against her pale pink skin. It was hard to take her in all at once, as though being apart required a new appreciation. I felt again what I had on the phone, a sense of the temporary. I told myself I viewed too much in life that way. Perhaps I should see us as a touchstone. I looked around. Not many people were walking; only a few students hurrying in the cold. An old man, the most distant figure, moved stiffly. Then it seemed right to think of us together. I realized that what she was was graceful, not beautiful. I looked down at her. A blue tweed pantsuit, flared, and three-quarter-length navy leather coat. It was expensive, and she was elegant. She didn't have prominent cheekbones. The planes of her face were angled along lines from her chin. Attractive and severe; seductive, too, I felt. In the cold sunlight her hair had a beautiful sheen, and as I took her in I knew I had missed her. She looked up at me, caught my eye, smiled and squeezed my hand inside my pocket.

Looking ahead of us, we went past the silent fountain. She said, "I never quit taking the pill."

"For Jake?" He was sixty-three, a bachelor who played viola in the quartet.

She laughed. "Yes, you fool. You never saw what was going on right in front of you."

"Not 'never.' I simply realized now."

"Some detective."

"Perhaps you should take your problems elsewhere, miss."

"I can't do that." She was serious, then smiling again. "Kiss me."

We were on the steps right above the lagoon, pressing against each other hard. The cars above us were a distant hum, until they were nothing at all.

"What shall we do this afternoon, Chris?"

"You've had lunch?"

"Yes."

"Let's go to my place."

She had a garage apartment in Cleveland Heights. We walked

back up the path we had just come down, past "The Thinker" and around the crunching gravel path to the museum parking lot. I took her back to her car, and we drove separately to her apartment.

It was surprising how large the apartment was; two big rooms, with a kitchen and a bathroom, all under a sloping roof that always made me wish it were raining. But the sun, warm on our legs, came through the thin white curtains of her bedroom the whole time we made love. Afterwards we lay naked on the sheets, silent in our pleasure with each other.

"Dave, will you go with me on the trip?" She rolled onto her right side, pressing against me, her left breast over my heart.

"I can't. I have a job." I had been waiting for the moment she would ask, and I had known I would lie, though I was less certain of the reason, since our separation now seemed nonexistent. I hadn't worked for a month. A small job in Columbus, looking for a runaway child, had been the last at the end of a good summer for me. "Besides, I thought you believed we should be independent."

"I do. But I've . . . I feel like making up for lost time." She rolled over on her back.

"We can until you leave." I looked over at her.

"That's not what I mean." She smiled slightly. "At least that's not all I mean. Are you afraid of a permanent attachment?"

"I don't think so. But that isn't what we intended."

We hadn't meant to become involved with each other, not on that night we met six months before, and that was how we had. We both knew we needed to be independent to do our work. So we accepted each other and made love, and fell in love.

But in September we had discovered that we had misjudged, or at least we became involved in self-recrimination, a sense that we had failed, each to the other, to live up to a bargain, and that each had become the bargain, the item. Maybe I viewed her as talented and too little else; maybe she had believed me completely independent. We misjudged because of what we admired, and because love joined that admiration.

One night after dinner at my apartment when we were undressing, she said she might quit performing.

"Why?" My surprise was in the one word.

"I don't feel happy with myself. I wanted to be first-rate."

"And you're not. Don't be foolish. Not every violinist can be Isaac Stern."

"Pull down this zipper for me." She had turned her back to avoid looking at me. "I'm not happy with . . . oh, I don't know . . . with my technique."

"I think it's great."

She pulled away so quickly that the nail of my index finger dug into my thumb. "Don't be smart."

"I take it back. Did you have a bad session?" She was hurt.

"It wasn't good."

"That's not enough to make you quit."

"No, it's not. But it's just the most recent of several bad rehearsals."

"I'm sure you exaggerate."

"Could you quit what you're doing?" She seemed overly earnest.

I hesitated, then, "Yes. But I've changed before, and I'm not the topic."

"All right, you're not, but what you've done is exactly what I'm talking about. That's the kind of independence I want." She stepped out of her dress and walked to the closet. "Why shouldn't I want it too?"

"Because you have a real ability that a bad rehearsal doesn't eliminate. You think I'm independent when I'm really alone. Don't change what I rely on. Don't you change."

She ignored my last remark. "What do you mean, alone?"

"I've learned to trust only myself. It just so happens that's as good a habit for a detective as the desire to know the truth. You're the only person I've trusted since I left my father's office."

She came over and kissed me. "You mean that, don't you? That must be very hard." She kissed me again. Instead of helping her, I'd made her reassure me. Maybe that had helped her.

We never talked of that night again, but the very qualities

that we admired, then loved, were undercut, ironically by themselves. That afternoon in November, as good as it was, was too soon to restate our relationship as we now knew it, so I lied to Chris and she went on tour without me. We spent the rest of that afternoon and night as though nothing had happened. Seemingly happy in love. A quick job checking references took me to Thanksgiving, but December was a blank. Still I didn't call Chris after she came back. Finally, I took a couple of hundred dollars out of the bank and went walking on the beach.

What was strange was the way I missed her—not at first, or continuously once the feeling arose, but intermittently and irrationally. I believed I loved her more than temporarily, that I needed her and she was good for me. I hoped I was so for her.

The day I walked from the lighthouse to the Cape it was raining, cold and penetrating, and I decided I couldn't quit, that what I was doing I had to do. If distrust was the wrong reason, it was necessary, and while I was not without belief, it had been tempered too often. Chris shouldn't change either, not because of me, or still less for me, because she was who she was.

So, when Mary asked me about Chris, the dull sky outside the restaurant reminded me of gray water and gray sky and the pall that lay on the world I worked in. But the gray waters beating each to each, becoming white, at the Cape had made me think of the two of us under a sloping roof.

"I haven't seen her for two months. She went on tour. I suppose she's back." My voice must have told what I felt. Mary didn't say any more about it and changed the subject.

She wanted to go Dutch when the bill came, but I felt a need to do something and refused her. About an hour after I got back to the office, Stedman called to say his mother and brother would both be home at three. Exactly twenty-four hours later I found myself back where the skeleton had been unearthed.

6

A heavy, wet snow, melting as it hit the ground, was falling when I drove up the hill to the Larch house. The sky had not changed. I'd been wrong on the possibility of snow, but a strong wind had come up, and if the temperature rose a few more degrees, there would be rain and ice instead of snow. I decided not to think that far ahead about something over which I had no control. Instead there were the next few unpleasant moments, which I might influence. Mrs. Larch, I suspected, would be the most difficult to talk with. Bob Stedman had said she still hated her husband. If so, she might not want to talk at all. Seeing Ben Larch first was the best approach. He might side with her, but I could appeal to his fair-mindedness first and possibly receive a more open hearing from her.

No sooner had I rung the bell than Bob Stedman opened the door. His face bright and eager, he seemed much surer of himself. The morose, heavy look of this morning had disappeared from the trim figure standing before me in a blue wool turtleneck and gray slacks. He was glad to see me and eager to start, so that any hope I had of seeing his mother and brother separately disappeared in his unwillingness to take my suggestion to see his brother first.

"Mother will see you the way she decides is best, not by what we think."

He pressed his hand on my shoulder as he moved me back to the library.

He made a clucking sound with his tongue when I asked where his mother was, so against my judgment, I let myself be directed. We entered the closed room without knocking, exactly opposite a desk where Ben Larch and his mother were working. The lamp on the desk cast a light just high enough for their surprise to be clearly illuminated. There was a pause in which no one spoke, only a matter of seconds, but to all but Bob it felt as long as the room was vast. Stedman's breathing was audible behind me. Again the pressure of his hand to impel me into the room, but I stood firm, forcing him to go around me. He moved out to the center of the room and made a slight gesture with his right hand, palm up, toward his mother.

"Mother, Mr. Stuart."

"I know." Her voice was firm, contrasting with his deference, which may not have been serious.

"Yes, of course; I meant he has something to tell you, to . . . apparently he's learned something since he was here yesterday." His voice was glib.

She had leaned back in her French Provincial armchair as he spoke. Her eyes shifted between the two of us and finally settled on me as he finished. Obviously, Stedman had not told her of our meeting and was now forcing me into a corner. Since that was the case, I wasn't going to have my hands tied, too.

"Mrs. Larch, I'm sorry to bother you, but I thought it might be useful if we talked."

"You could have made an appointment"—she looked at Bob—"but I'm free to see you now. Ben and I were just going over some antiques catalogues. He'll probably be going to London next month to make several purchases for the business." She smiled at Ben. "What can we do for you, now that you are here?" She preferred to say nothing of Bob's arrangement to bring us together.

"I may as well be direct, Mrs. Larch. In making some inquiries, I learned that you were married to a Paul Stedman after Mr. Larch died."

"Have my private affairs some particular interest for you,

Mr. Stuart?" A slight smile flickered on her lips and disappeared; she maintained control of herself. She stood up and walked to the couch where she had sat yesterday. The clothes were still simple and expensive: a blue wool suit with white collar and cuffs, a small diamond pin. I thought her clothing indicated that she could deal with any contingency.

"Not directly. But someone paid me a retainer to look into the discovery of the body yesterday. That was how I found out."

She looked from her younger son to the older, but remained expressionless.

"I don't see where my mother's marriages are connected." Larch walked over to stand between his mother and me.

"Probably they don't have any connection, but I wondered if it occurred to you yesterday that the skeleton may have been that of Mr. Stedman."

"Oh, come on now, Stuart. There must be dozens of unsolved disappearances."

"Now, now, Ben. I think I understand Mr. Stuart's line of thought. After all, the skeleton was found on our property." Her voice was soothing and assured.

I looked over at Stedman, who had a fixed smile on his face. I had a feeling he was admiring his mother, approving her admonishment.

"Thank you, Mrs. Larch. Your son is right about disappearances, but I thought, as you seem to realize, that I should start with one close to the place of discovery."

"Exactly." She was about to go on when Stedman interrupted her.

"Is that all you had in mind?" His voice wasn't as hostile as Larch's was, and his mother looked at him earnestly, without reproof, as though fathoming his purpose.

"Yes." I was angry that he tipped my hand but made my answer as toneless as possible.

"I think Mr. Stuart and I should have a private talk, if you will excuse us."

Ben said, "Of course." Bob said nothing. Both left immediately.

She walked to the window, after seeing the door close behind them.

"Perhaps it won't rain after all. I hope not. The ice is so hard on the trees. Two years after Bob's father left me, we had a bad ice storm." She turned back from the window. "A power line on the main road was broken. For a child that's an adventure— I remember Bob—but not for me." She sat down and I took the corner of the couch across the table from her.

"What did Bob tell you?" Now we were open. I had to admire her directness.

"I think you deserve an answer, but you may be surprised at how little I know. He said his father left you ten years ago for his partner's wife. That the partner died two months later in a plane crash and that after a year you obtained a divorce."

"Did he tell you I hate his father?" I was amazed by the calm voice that revealed almost no feeling.

"Do you now?"

"More than ever." Still the same flat voice.

"You don't sound as though you do."

"Would flying into a rage be more convincing? Possibly. Believe it or not, I hadn't thought of the possibility of that being my husband's skeleton. I wouldn't feel any remorse if it were, but I find no pleasure in vituperation."

"You hated him enough to kill him?"

"Yes, but I didn't."

"And time hasn't healed."

"Not this. If he were dead, if I knew that was his body, I could forget. But as long as he lives, he shames me." For the first time, when she referred to herself, the tone I anticipated appeared.

"Could you kill?"

"That is not a kind question, but neither is this conversation. Yes, I could. I think most people can. Surely you have seen that in your work." Then the afterthought, "And I have lived long enough to know it is true."

I didn't answer this point. "Did you try to find him?"

"Yes. I hired a detective. One my lawyer recommended. For a while he seemed to be hard at work. At least he cost enough."

The reference to money surprised me, for she didn't have any apparent worry. It was the clearest sign that she begrudged any act for her husband. "He stopped abruptly, about six months after he started."

"Did he come to see you when he quit?"

"No. The last thing I received was a letter from some little town in Massachusetts. That was all."

"Do you still have the letter?"

She smiled at me as though I were feebleminded. "Do you think I would keep that for nearly ten years?"

"You might."

"Some people might. I didn't. I kept it for a while, along with the other reports, but when I decided not to pursue the search, I kept them only until the divorce was settled, then threw them out." She sighed. "I suppose Paul paid him off, though God knows how."

"Did he have money of his own?"

"Not much. Not as much as Mr. Roscoe would know I could pay."

"What was the detective's name?"

"Dwight. Dwight Roscoe."

"Do you remember the postmark of his last letter?"

"Pittsfield, Massachusetts."

"Do you remember any of it?"

"No. As I recall, all of his reports were very general—where he was, why there."

"Possibly his leads were unsuccessful. Am I disturbing you with these questions?"

"Of course you are. But I said I could understand your reasons, and now I want to know if the body is Paul's."

"And you have guessed that Bob hired me?"

"Yes. The moment I saw you together at the door. He had to have hired you."

"Have you followed that through?"

She nodded. "Naturally, it means he knew about the skeleton."

"Only that something was buried there."

"Are you sure?"

"Here." I gave her the Xerox copy of the letter, having decided to trust her not to go to the police.
"Where did Bob get this?"
"From Alec Bolen."
"Alec? How did he get it?"
"Apparently in the mail. Ten years ago."
"Ten years. Then Paul may have put the body there, too."
"Possibly. But whom would he kill?"
"Anyone. Shouldn't the police see this?"
"Yes. But first I wanted to show it to some people—including you—on my own. Your son came to me, so I felt I owed him that much." I wasn't going to tell her how I felt about Carlson and his professionalism.
"I see. Well, I won't say anything. Frankly, I've always felt guilty about Bob. After his father left, I found it very hard to love him. He was the one sign of that mistake I had not been able to obliterate. I'm afraid it's affected him ever since. He's really a very shy boy, and he's never been made to feel loved. He knew after the divorce that I hated his father, and I think he's known it ever since." She put her left hand on the table in a gesture that appeared to be reaching. "Have you wondered why he isn't in school? He's just twenty-one."
"I know."
"He should be a senior, but he barely finished his sophomore year. He hasn't been in college in over a year now. I may hate his father, but I feel sorry for him."
I did too. For there was no love in what she said, only a vague sense of charity, expressed in the same bland, controlled tone she used to describe her hate. She would provide for him and protect him, but offer little more.
"I won't tell the police. That can be your decision. Maybe Bob needs a man with whom to identify. He and Ben have never been close."
I simply nodded and took my lead from her last words.
"Were you and Paul close?"
She nodded. "Once. Paul was younger than I. Ambitious and energetic. I was thirty-seven, he was thirty. Ben, my first hus-

band, had just died in an automobile accident and I was very lonely."

"No family?"

"My son and my mother, but she was almost eighty. I'm an only child. Ben and I both had inherited money, but not Paul. That never mattered to me. We met at a party. A year later we were married. Those first ten years weren't bad. The first few were good. We once loved each other. At least I loved him. I even helped establish him in business. He'd met Bill Penn, who sold him on the idea of the shops. I wish they'd never heard of each other, and for the short while he lived, I'm sure Penn wished so too." She paused, perhaps aware that she expressed more feeling over her second marriage than she had revealed before, or intended. "Have you ever been in love?"

I nodded.

"Then you may understand how I felt. Why I hated Paul so, and still do."

She probably hoped for an answer. Her blue eyes fixed on my face, then moved away when I did not reply. Reality was that to hate for ten years, as to mourn for as long, was at best an obsession. But to suggest so was worse than useless, so I remained silent.

"He shamed me. First he used me, then he shamed me. What was there to do but go back to my original name, Ben's name? It was still good. Ben was a good man. He might have been a great one had he lived. He could have been governor or senator. His grandfather was a senator."

She laughed, high, almost shrill. "Mixed marriages don't work."

"What do you mean?"

"Mixed marriages—Paul's and mine. He was poor, I'm rich. Ben and I were both wealthy."

She had been talking long enough to break through her reserve, at least to a layer of self-pity, an area most of us find easily. It might have been wiser to leave her then, but she might realize later that she had revealed a small part of herself—a very small part—that she intended to keep private and would refuse to see me again. I sat perfectly still, facing her. Her pause went on, so I decided to fill it.

"Who was Bill Penn?"

"No one special. He never said much about himself, but I gathered he had some kind of sales or public relations background."

I thought she knew more than she said.

"Yet you lent money to your husband to go into business."

"I could afford it. And I didn't lend." Her tone was emphatic. "I gave Paul the money. Paul had worked in sales before, so I trusted the idea of some clothing shops—boutiques."

"That's what they had?"

"Three of them. Two on the east side, one on the west. It's been a good idea; Alec Bolen can tell you." She smiled again when she mentioned his name.

"Did you know Mrs. Penn?"

"Ellen? Not really. She was pretty, in a way; late twenties. A few years younger than Bill." Or Paul, I thought to myself.

"Do you know how she and your husband met?"

"No. Perhaps she had a greater interest in the business than I did." The distant, neutral tone had returned to her voice. "They depended on the money; I didn't." She made the last sound like a simple fact, but it still had a chill, dreary undercurrent for me.

"Did you see Bill Penn after your husband left you?"

"Yes, twice. The day after we were deserted, he came out here. We weren't much good for each other. We were both enraged. I blamed him for not watching her. I was unfair. About a month later—no, maybe it was two, closer to the time he died—he came to see me about arranging for Paul's share of the profits. I told him to see Alec. As I recall, we parted amicably. Poor Bill."

She got up and crossed to the window again.

"I was right; it isn't going to rain. The snow is beginning to stick to the branches. It's lovely." She turned to me. "Don't you agree?"

"Yes, it is."

"I think I've told you everything I know. I'm rather pleased with myself." She made a tight line that turned upward with her mouth. There was self-satisfaction, and I was not going to be let in.

"Did your husband have any enemies?"

"That's melodramatic. Not that I know of, but I didn't know most of the people he dealt with. As I said, I think I've told you all I can."

I stood, she extended her hand and we said good afternoon, all in a polite, formal way that was in keeping with our conversation and with the tone she obviously wished to reestablish. As we started to the door she touched my left arm.

"You see that vase?" She spoke the word with at least two h's. "It's exquisite, isn't it?" As trite as the word exquisite can be, she made it sound like the only correct word. "Late Ming." It was a small vase with musicians enameled over a blue underglaze. "My grandmother acquired it seventy-five years ago. It's over four hundred years old. Things of value last, don't they?"

"Yes . . . they do." I wondered if she realized the possibilities of what she said. I thought of myself.

"You've been very helpful, and more than generous with your time, Mrs. Larch." I decided she wanted to end on a calm note, and so I let her down gently, as she seemed to request. She said good-by again at the library door and remained behind.

I was slightly surprised to find both Stedman and Larch in the front hall, on straight-backed chairs that faced each other from opposite sides of the front door. Larch was angry, barely under control. Stedman was whistling "Pop! Goes the Weasel." He stopped with calculated surprise at my appearance, as though I were the last person he expected to see come out of the library. A smirk irritated the hell out of me, and I imagined how the two had baited each other while waiting.

Larch walked over to me while I was still staring at Stedman. "How is my mother?"

"Yes, how is she?" Stedman put in before I could reply. He behaved as though in a British drawing room comedy.

"Shut up, Bob. Shut the hell up."

"Tch, tch." Bob said no more, but went upstairs. When he was halfway up he started to whistle the tune again. We could hear him until a door closed. I was puzzled that his anxious curiosity could be so controlled now as to let him walk away. More than likely he didn't want to talk in front of his brother.

"Could I talk to you for a while? Do you have some time?" Ben was flustered. "I need to calm down a bit. But I do have some questions."

"Sure. Where shall we go to talk?"

He looked around fretfully, then said, "Let's go down to my place."

We retrieved our coats from the closet and set out down the driveway. The snow was still falling in big wet flakes which tried to cover everything. The woods forming a perimeter to the lawn were gray through the distance of heavy flakes. Falling heavily, the snow made no whirling clouds of cold dust. The roof of the house was covered, and our tracks, like our coats, were rapidly obliterated in white. The woods behind the house were reached through the Larch garage courtyard. From inside, the house had appeared situated at the brink of a hill; from without I could see the sharp descent. In the woods the trees took on sharp contrasts of black bark and white snow. Clean opposites. Larch led the way silently, evidently attempting to recover his composure. We started down a series of gently sloping switchbacks, lighted every five yards or so with low ground lamps, like large black beetles on single legs. In a better season I imagined the hillside was covered in azaleas and wildflowers.

We had walked several hundred feet back and forth, but only about seventy-five feet down, when through the white and black of the woods I saw the house, perhaps fifty feet below us. Looking back up the hill, the original house was a shape broken here and there by lights. The settings and the houses could contrast no more radically. Larch's redwood and glass house was spread along the hillside, and cantilevered out from the slope unnaturally. Despite its smaller size, its position was tenuous when compared to his mother's house.

"Leslie may not be home yet. She was going to look after her collies." We were on a walkway which extended from the hillside to a covered entry.

"You have an unusual house."

"Does that mean modern doesn't appeal to you?" He tried to smile, and I felt the difficulty was not in the subject of the house.

"On the contrary, it does, and I only meant what I said. It must have been difficult to build."

"It was, to preserve the hillside and bring in the materials. A lot of the hill had to be replanted, but we saved every large tree." We were at the front door; he looked back up the hill. "Only the underbrush had to be landscaped, and now you wouldn't be able to tell. Come in."

We entered an enormous foyer, its slate floor running in three directions—to the living room and down halls to the left and right. He hung our coats in the closet, then led the way into the living room. An enormous curved window twenty-five feet long made the outside wall. A fireplace was near the middle of the inside wall on my right, a copper hood extending over the brick hearth.

"I need a drink; can I get you one?"

"Scotch with a little water."

He used a wet bar behind a panel at the left end of the room. I looked over the leather, chrome and plastic furniture, the oriental rugs—none as large as the one in his mother's study—on the polished wide-planked oak floor. The Larches knew how to spend their money. Expensive but restrained was the common denominator of the two houses.

"Here." He handed me a low glass packed with ice and Scotch. He gestured toward the wall at the opposite end of the room. "I keep the modern works for myself and sell the things my mother likes. I'm not much of an investor, but they are my bets on long-range appreciation."

"I've heard a lot of people speculate in art, that it only appreciates."

"That's generally true, though one must know a few things to make the right purchases. Let's sit down." He led the way to some Barcelona chairs by the window. The snow continued to fall. In the trees the darkness was growing complete.

"I'm sorry for the scene you caught up there. I'm glad my mother missed it."

"Was that what you wanted to tell me?"

He smiled faintly. "No, of course not. Actually, I was hoping you would tell me what you asked my mother."

"You have some idea already?"

"Yes. You learned about Bob's father."

I was convinced that, like his mother, he had been waiting since yesterday for Paul Stedman's name to make its appearance. Obviously the past was hard to forget, yet neither wished to have it surface.

"Don't you and your mother speak to each other?"

He seemed surprised, then simply raised his eyebrows. "We're very close, very." He paused. "But if there is one thing we don't talk about, it's her second husband. That's why Bob and I quarreled." He snorted and took a long pull at his glass. "He should have told us first."

"But you just said that couldn't have been a surprise."

"That my brother would bring you was."

"Perhaps that's as much my fault as his." I didn't mention how Bob had anxiously pushed me back to the library. "I was surprised that you wouldn't tell me something as important as the fact that a husband was missing. That the body might be his."

"It didn't cross my mind, at least not yesterday." His voice modulated smoothly, under control now.

"Did you mention this to your mother?"

"No, never. There was no reason to trouble her with my suspicions." He swallowed a mouthful of Scotch.

"How do you and your brother get along?"

"We hardly ever see each other. In some ways I've had to play father to him. I'm almost fifteen years older than he is, and when Paul abandoned my mother, I was the oldest man left. The only one." He shook his head. "And now that I think of it, I was only a little older than Bob is now."

"But how do you get along?"

"You're persistent." He smiled as if to let me know he wasn't angry. "We're not very close. But we aren't usually at each other's throats the way you saw us now. The fact is we have little to do with each other." He put his drink on a low chromed steel and glass Parsons table, then reached for his shirt pocket. "Do you care for a cigarette?" He withdrew his hand and snapped his fingers before I answered, excused himself and started for the kitchen.

As he returned he opened the pack, carefully folding back the foil paper from one side of the seal and tamping a cigarette out by rapping the pack on the knuckle of the index finger of the left hand.

"Here." He extended the pack.

"No, thanks; I finally managed to quit."

"I wish I could." He pulled the cigarette for himself and snapped open an initialed Zippo. He waved his hand back over his head in a stream of smoke. "I have quit smoking at my mother's. I started about ten years ago, but she never approved."

"About the time your stepfather disappeared."

"There was no connection." Then he laughed, breaking the solemnity with which he spoke of the past. "Unless it is symbolic. No, I started when I went into the business. The auctions, the bidding and bickering. Trying to please a client when I can't find the desired object at the desired time and price. I had to smoke or go batty. But I like what I do—I really do." He seemed not only relieved but pleased to talk about his work. And he wanted me to know.

"Certainly there must be some pleasure in being your own man. I get some of that feeling myself."

"Yes, of course, you would understand. Of course I have the advantage of regular clients—heaven forbid customers—while you go from one person to another."

"When I'm lucky. I'm sure your business is more regular than mine." I sipped the Scotch, holding it in my mouth before swallowing. I should have known it would be premium and was sorry to have asked for water. We both passed some quiet seconds with our drinks. Larch was abstracted, as though seriously comparing our jobs; then he shook himself free self-consciously.

"I'm sorry. My mind wandered for a moment. You must have an interesting life."

"Occasionally, but not very often."

"Anyway, we were discussing my brother and me." He sighed as he voluntarily returned to the subject, "I've felt sorry for Bob, the wasted time, the absence of a father. He missed over a year of college and, as you might guess, is out of college now. He has nothing to do and nothing he seems to want to do."

"Did his father's desertion depress him?"

"Yes and no, at least at the time. He didn't know what had happened, and he was confused when his father wasn't there." He paused, inhaled deeply on the cigarette. "It was a lousy thing his father did."

"To him?"

"To all of us."

"And you were here when it happened?"

"Yes." He smiled comfortably. "Except for college, I have always lived here."

"What were you two quarreling about?"

"Just now?"

I nodded.

He pursed his lips. "I made the mistake of criticizing Paul Stedman. Bob seems to think he's alive, or that if he's dead he's going to find his killer. He's obsessed."

"He isn't completely wrong. There was a letter from his father a couple of weeks ago."

"He didn't tell me." His eyes squinted in disbelief.

"Here, read this." I unfolded the copy and gave it to him. He put out his cigarette. He read it rapidly and then again more slowly.

"It's ten years old . . . and anyone could have written it." He measured his words after his surprise. "But I see why Bob's upset. He's the one who hired you."

I nodded. "And don't tell the police yet. Your mother has seen the letter and agreed not to discuss it with them."

"Of course. If that is what she wants." He slapped his forehead. "Is there anything I can do? God, I used some harsh words about Paul."

"Weasel one of them?"

"I think so." He was shaking his head. "Why?"

"Bob was whistling."

"Yes . . . yes." He walked to the window and peered into the growing darkness, looking down the hillside to the west. He made no effort to turn on a light. "I was looking for Leslie. Is this what you were telling my mother?"

"Yes."

"So I'm the last to know."

"What little there is to tell." I finished my drink and put my glass opposite his on the glass tabletop. "Actually, I'm glad you wanted to talk. I thought you might tell me something your mother forgot or preferred not to think about. The subject might be easier for you to handle."

"Yes, of course. It's not pleasant, but I can handle it better than Mother can." He picked up his glass but didn't drink. We were in almost total darkness, yet he still didn't turn on the lights. The ice clinked in his glass.

"What kind of business did your stepfather have?"

"A partnership in some clothing stores—women's clothing. He was onto the idea of British imports just as they were becoming popular."

"Was the idea his?"

"Penn's, I think. Bill Penn had the idea and the connections. Paul had the capital, or at least my mother did."

"What did Stedman do before opening the shops?"

"He worked in sales in one of the family companies—Inter-Lake Ore. It was one of my grandfather's holdings that Mother inherited intact." He raised his glass and the ice slid forward.

"Your mother made the place for him?"

"Yes."

"Why did he want to leave?"

"To be on his own." Larch's voice was cold. "Even though he needed money."

"Was it a loan?"

"He never paid any money back."

"Could he?"

"Yes, there were good profits, as I recall, but he didn't."

"Would your mother let him?"

"I don't see why not."

56

I wondered if she would. She had said not, but with time, one's side becomes more just. "How much was involved?"
"Over one hundred thousand." He pulled out another cigarette and let the lighter illuminate his face before shutting us up in darkness again. "Leslie is really late. Perhaps I should go down to the kennels."
"Do you want to?"
"No, she'll be okay. What else did you want to know?"
"What kind of person was Penn?"
"I can't say I knew him. I was about twenty-three. He was ten years or so older, younger than Paul."
"What were you doing at the time?"
He laughed lightly. "Working for Inter-Lake."
"Sales?"
"Yes, I suppose I did see the change coming. That Paul wanted something else."
"Like you later."
"Yes, I suppose we both wanted to try to prove something on our own. Only he deceived us."
"And was it possible to see the deception coming?"
"Paul did a lot with the Penns after the business was set up. Ellen ran one of the stores. She was young enough to fit the stores' image. Occasionally the three of them made buying trips together. I don't know how Paul and Ellen Penn got mixed up together—they fooled us."
"Us?"
"Our family." There was surety in his voice.
"Was she attractive?"
"Yes. No question about that. She flaunted herself."
"Did she and her husband ever quarrel?"
"I never saw any differences between them."
"How about your mother and stepfather?"
The front door opened and the hall light went on.
"We're in here, Leslie."
"Who's with you?"
"Mr. Stuart."
"What are you doing in the dark?" There was the amusement in her voice.

"Waiting for you." He was irritated by her tone. "I thought I might see you on the hill if the light wasn't on."

All the while she was hanging up her coat and removing her boots with a metallic clicking and wet slapping.

"It's snowing harder." She threw a switch as she came down the steps, and lights recessed in the ceiling came on. We both blinked at the brightness. Her face was flushed, and she looked younger than she had yesterday. Drops of water hung in her hair, remnants of snow. Her jeans were wet and her sweatshirt bagged over her hips. She came over to kiss her husband. "I had to wait for a man to come about Laird."

"You smell like a dog." He was serious.

She only smiled. "Shouldn't I, after three hours? I'll clean up. Mr. Stuart, will you stay for another drink?"

"Certainly."

"I'll hurry." She ran from the room. He watched her go, then looked at me. He was angry, but repressed it with a small upward movement at the right side of his mouth.

"Those dogs take too much of her time. We could afford a full-time trainer." He wasn't reminding me of their money, but thinking aloud. "Where were we?"

"You said you never saw the Penns quarrel."

"Only over her general seductiveness."

"What happened?"

"I don't remember. That's not something I want to remember."

"What about Penn's background? Did you ever check it?"

"Naturally it was checked. I didn't have anything to do with that, however."

Mrs. Larch did know more about Penn than she had told me, and it was unlikely she had forgotten.

"But you did later."

He leaned back against the leather cushion and folded his arms. "Yes, I saw the record when the business was sold. He didn't have a credit rating, only an employment record. There was nothing unusual that I recall."

"Had he been in business for himself before?"

"A motel in Florida . . . but he sold that before coming here."

The photo of Bob and his father flitted across my brain.

"Yet he had no capital to put up, only the idea?"

"That's right. You think he held something out?"

"Possibly. What if that was your stepfather's skeleton? And what if he never did run away with Ellen Penn, if he was dead the whole time?"

"But Penn died in a plane crash."

"That could be bad luck. There's a more serious problem to the theory. How would they have profited? What could they gain?"

He shrugged and shook his head. "I don't know. No one made a claim on the business. I never paid any attention to it, and I don't think Mother did either. We let Alec handle everything."

"It's a distinct possibility that the Penns conspired against your stepfather. I'll have to talk to Alec Bolen about the business. How about your mother and stepfather? Did they get along?" I came back to what I wanted to know.

"Shouldn't you ask my mother?" He uncrossed his arms and laid them by his sides.

"I did, but she wasn't very specific."

"Would you like another drink?"

I shook my head.

"I think I'll have another one." He walked behind me to the bar. "Perhaps she didn't feel it was your business."

"Perhaps. But I would think the family would like to know the truth."

"We did want to know. We hired a detective." The ice clinked into his glass. The whisky splashed from the bottle.

"I know. But when he disappeared you made no further attempts."

"No. If they had hidden successfully for six months, we assumed they couldn't be found." He came back to his chair, keeping his glass in his hand.

"That doesn't make much sense. Why search to begin with?"

"To get the divorce, but Mother wanted the search stopped when the detective failed to report again after six months. I think it should be her right."

"Hadn't she and her husband been getting along well?"

"I was right when I said you were persistent. It's not your business, but no, not for at least two years before he left." He was using the same voice he had when his wife had come in.

"That was before he met Penn."

"Yes." He lifted his glass.

"Did they quarrel?"

"Some. Over her money. He wanted more independence." He took another swallow. "As if he would have been anything without our money." It was the first bitterness I'd heard—all there in his voice.

"You have some strong feelings about him."

"Yes. More than usual. But then I don't usually talk about him."

"More than your mother has."

"That is the difference between us. She has poise . . . grace."

"Who's that?" It was his wife. She stood on the steps, fastening the clasp of a bracelet. She had on a green cashmere cardigan and blue and green plaid slacks.

"Mother."

She merely nodded and smiled at his reply. "Could you get me a drink, Ben?"

He did as asked, and she walked over to me and took her husband's chair. He returned with a martini on the rocks, handed it to her, then pulled up a bentwood rocking chair.

"You ought to stay, Mr. Stuart; the snow is falling harder than ever." I liked her smile, for it was the only one to make me truly welcome.

"No, I don't want to intrude further than I have."

We had been watching each other, but I took a quick look at Larch to see what his feelings were. He was stolid.

"No, you wouldn't be. I was going to fix stroganoff, and I have everything cut up." She turned to her husband. "You see, Ben, I do make some plans to suit you. I knew you would want dinner on time." He said nothing.

"Thank you anyway, but I should get home before we're snowbound."

"Why don't you start dinner?" Ben paused, his intent clear; then he smiled from her to me. "Perhaps Mr. Stuart will stay when he smells your stroganoff."

She sat deliberately for a moment, sipped the martini; then without speaking went toward the kitchen. He rocked silently, watching her go. He waited until a cabinet door closed, then he looked at me.

"Sorry for the interruption, but it gave me a chance to cool off. I never liked Paul. He was an intruder who thought he had a right to everything. He was never more than an impecunious interloper with charm. The longer I knew him, the more certain I was. So you see why I'm not interested in stirring up the past and upsetting my mother." He took out a cigarette and moved to his original chair. He lighted up and spoke as he exhaled, "That is why Bob and I quarreled. I suppose it's a kind of jealousy between half-brothers that can't be healed. But I do feel sorry for him. To live, knowing what his father did." He snapped the cigarette at an enameled ashtray.

I tapped my fingers on the table. "I'd better have a talk with Alec Bolen."

"Yes, he can tell you more about the business."

"And you don't object?"

"Of course not." Then, "Would it matter?"

"Probably. He would be more helpful if he knew you agreed."

"Tell him I do, by all means." He inhaled deeply, as though sighing. "Tell him to call me if he wants confirmation."

"Thank you for your time, and the drink."

We got up and walked to the entry. Leslie's plain black rubber boots stood in a puddle on the slate, some feces softened by the water stuck to the side of the left one. I caught Larch's glance—they were an intrusion, an insult. He helped me on with my topcoat and opened the door for me. When I'd crossed the bridge to the hillside I heard the

soft plop of the boots in the snow on the deck behind me.
The giant beetles glowed, some of them almost entirely covered by the snow. I slipped once on the way up, thought I should have stayed, then was glad I hadn't. The lights appeared and disappeared through the trees, making angled layers back up the hillside. By the time I saw the lights in the house above, I was halfway up; my coat was almost white and wet and the lights below were out. One light was on upstairs, while several first-floor rooms were lighted. I made fresh tracks through the garage courtyard, brushed off my coat and the windshield as well as possible, and drove off through the dismal night.

On the freeway I passed several minor accidents. It took me three hours to get home. Most of that time the words kept going through my head—impecunious interloper—and I wondered when Ben Larch began to think of his stepfather in that way.

7

By morning six inches of snow clung to everything that didn't move, and to most of the few things that did. The eight o'clock news ran a list of schools closed and streets to avoid. The snow had stopped falling and the temperature was going to hover near freezing. With any luck, life could flow as usual by evening. Then I told myself that yesterday afternoon I thought it was going to rain. I should stick to the possible. Still forty-five minutes before I would try Bolen. Another cup of instant coffee and the paper filled the time. The headless skeleton was on the second page, in the lower left-hand corner. Good. I put the dishes in the dish washer and looked up Bolen's office.

Bolen wasn't just the lawyer for the Larches. He sat on boards and advised politicians, a new Mark Hanna. Few people had heard his name; I had, through my father, who had known him for twenty years. Bolen could have lived on his assets; even one of his consultations would keep an upper-middle-class family for a year. But he would be at work if the roads were passable, because he lived a work ethic as seriously as any nineteenth-century industrialist. His earnestness must have transferred to the office staff, because I reached a receptionist who gave me his secretary who took my name.

"Mr. Bolen is busy right now. Can I have him return your call?"

"How long would that be?"

"I can't say, Mr. Stuart. He's very busy." Obviously the storm hadn't affected efficiency.

"Is he with a client?"

She hesitated long enough for me to know he wasn't.

"Could you simply give him my name? He'll know it. Perhaps he would tell when he might return the call."

She hesitated again; then the line went short. It worked, because the next voice was friendly and male.

"Jack, how are you?"

"This is David Stuart, Mr. Bolen. You know my father."

"Yes, of course." He was more formal, but not angry. "How is your father?"

"He's fine. I'm calling about a mutual client."

"Are you still working as a detective?"

"Yes."

"Well, whom are we sharing, David?" The first name might have been for my father's sake, but it was more likely that he was establishing his seniority with the client.

"The Larches."

"You're working on the skeleton case? For whom?"

"Robert Stedman, the younger son."

"I see." There was no surprise in his voice at any of my answers. It was just possible that once since yesterday morning he had allowed himself to think that Bob and the letter were linked to the skeleton. Then he would have put the thought aside.

"I've talked with both Mrs. Larch and her other son, too. Ben Larch knows I'm calling you today."

Again, "I see."

"Would it be possible to meet today?"

"Let me look at my calendar." There was a pause of several seconds. "I'm busy all morning. But why don't we have lunch? If it weren't business, I'd have your father join us."

"That sounds good to me. When and where should I meet you?"

"Around one at Stouffer's on the square."

"Fine. Thank you."

So far, okay. He was guarded but friendly. If he purposefully wanted an informal meeting, there was no reason to decline.

The main streets were passable, masses of slush and dirty water. Winter was only a reminder of how filthy the city had become: the air visibly saturated with exhaust, the snow blackened by soot and dust. I didn't go to the office but parked off West 3rd to keep our appointment. Though I was five minutes early, he was already waiting. We shook hands and I hung up my coat.

Bolen was in his sixties, about five-eight, with thick white hair that was fashionably long. To see him was to know he was successful—in a dark gray, blue pin-striped suit, blue shirt, red and blue silk tie—but not to suspect that he was as prominent as he was. I knew he was seeing me because of the Larch family name, which even he respected. The situation, I suspected, was more personal for him than it was yet for me.

We talked idly about the weather and my father, without having a drink ordered lunch, and finally, against a background of clicking knives and forks and the murmur of conversation, began to talk over what had brought us together.

"Robert called you because of the letter I delivered to him."

"Yes." I told him of the retainer, the police, and my first meeting with Bob. "He was obviously frightened and lacked the curiosity, because of his fear, to dig by himself."

"I can't say I blame him. Can you?" He buttered a roll.

"No. The letter you turned over to him was peculiarly impersonal. I think that any voice from the past would be frightening, and this one lacked a tone."

He drank some water, then asked, "Do you have the letter with you?"

"Here's a copy." While he read it I ate a roll and watched him. He read it slowly.

"Do you think Stedman sent it?" I asked.

"It's from the same typewriter that the cover directions were typed on."

"Do you have that letter?"

He smiled. "Yes, also a copy. I thought you might want to see it." He returned my copy, then his own.

The letter was equally simple.

December 1967

Dear Mr. Bolen:
Enclosed is a letter for my son, Robert Stedman. Please deliver it to him on his twenty-first birthday. I hope the enclosed one hundred dollars will cover your services.

Paul M. Stedman

"Sent locally?"

"Yes. Ten years ago."

"Since they are unsigned, we have no way of knowing he wrote either letter."

"And probably never will. Unless you get lucky."

"I don't think it will be luck, Mr. Bolen. Someone wants us to find Paul Stedman—whether Stedman himself or not, whether he's the skeleton or not. Otherwise, I see no purpose to the letters. But why wait for ten years to start the search? Why plan to have a search made ten years in advance?"

"If you mean for me to answer those questions, I can't. And I prefer not to speculate. That, I'm glad to say, is your problem. Once I gave that letter to Robert, I had no responsibility." He smiled as he spoke, genuinely pleased to be out of the way. Now I realized why he wanted to meet outside his office; this wasn't going to be his business.

"What about the detective you recommended?"

"Who was that?"

A waitress put an individual shrimp casserole in front of him and a ham sandwich and soup before me.

"Dwight Roscoe."

He broke the browned surface of the casserole, and steam rose. "He never finished the case. As a matter of fact he never came back. That surprised me, because I'd always found him reliable, absolutely trustworthy."

"Then you had used him before?"

"Occasionally. He usually did character references for me, but he told me he had done missing persons cases before, so when Mrs. Larch wanted someone, he seemed a suitable choice. I don't remember what she was paying, but doubtless he could have used a large fee."

I ignored the personal implications. "Did you look for him when he disappeared?"

"He wasn't working directly for me at the time." There was no smile this time, but I could see that if Bolen was able to remain uninvolved he would, as a matter of policy, perhaps principle. It was the way to confidences and power—not very pleasant, but reliable. We looked at each other; then I took some water to clear my mouth.

"What about the business that Stedman and Penn had? What became of it?"

He smiled and wiped the right corner of his mouth with his napkin. I popped the last bite of half a sandwich into my mouth.

"It's flourishing." Then a mocking frown. "But only after it nearly went under."

Surprised that he knew, I asked, "What happened?"

"I bought it." He smiled and shook his head slightly. "Not for myself—for my daughter." His voice warmed to his subject. "She was twenty, a dropout. Frankly, I was afraid of what she would do. Since I could afford it, I bought the business."

"And"—smiling as pleasantly as I could—"what about your conflict of interest? Weren't you representing the Larches?"

"Your father represented them."

"My father!"

"Yes. He handles that size estate regularly."

"You asked him to, so that you could purchase the company?"

"Partnership. I bought half a partnership then."

"What about that point—since there was no proof of Stedman's death?" An attractive blonde, laughing at something the man she was with said, bumped my arm with her hip. The water in the glass I was holding swayed to clicking ice. She kept on walking.

"That was an attractive girl. You . . . I wish I were young again." He shook his head. "What were you asking?" I was certain he had heard me, but I repeated myself.

He held his fork above his plate. "That was somewhat

tangled. Penn was dead, but, you see, his wife wasn't to inherit the business. Stedman simply wasn't here. After a little more than a year your father demonstrated that an adequate search had been made. . . ."

"Roscoe?"

"Yes. And that hardship would result if an absentee trustee was not appointed."

"During that year the business nearly disappeared. Actually we needed to wait only three months, but Roscoe's search went on. The store managers couldn't do any coherent bargaining for merchandise. They needed direction."

"But how could he sell the assets?"

"Again he had a right to protect the heirs. Penn had a brother; Robert was the other heir. When I offered more than it was worth, since they were going under, there was every reason to approve the sale. Actually I bought only half the partnership at first. Penn's brother is an airline pilot on the West Coast and had no interest in the business, so he sold for the straight cash. Then, about two years later the offer was upped, and your father advised Robert to sell. Your father did the right thing for the boy. You needn't think it was dishonest."

The borderline aspects of the case were distasteful but legal. My father would never harm a client's interests, either. I couldn't believe that.

I was sure Bolen knew the right people, too. "Why did you want that business, particularly if it was foundering? Not just for the stores."

"Frankly, because of the franchises it owned. My daughter was the one who told me that they might be worth a great deal. She said Stedman and Penn were right about the British influence in clothes. She was right."

"I'll say." I finished my coffee. Bolen strained the remaining shrimp with his fork.

"We franchised several of the brand names, even the name of the store itself—The Purple Tree. Isn't that awful?" He smiled to himself.

"Not as bad as some I've seen since. You said we."

"I'm a legal advisor, but that's all. Sandy is too independent to need me. Besides, she has a husband to help her . . . has had for the last six years. Shrewd fellow, too; diversified the stores with other imports—German and Scandinavian. And got them into accessories and household items. But you don't need to hear about that."

"No, on the contrary. I am interested. I wouldn't go into the business, but I'm curious about its operation."

"There's nothing very special to describe. They took the franchises already held, bought others and expanded into a chain. They'll sell the whole store to a reliable buyer and keep his books, or simply franchise a single line of merchandise. It's an ordinary enough franchise operation."

"Except that it's one of the successful ones that isn't selling hamburgers and chicken."

He laughed. "Exactly."

"Too bad for Stedman he didn't know what he was walking out on."

"He must have had some idea or he never would have gotten into the work."

"Did you know Penn?"

"No. But he was apparently the one with the merchandising connections. Stedman had access to money, but no real influence over the business."

"Do you mean he must have had a good reason to leave it, to throw a position over?"

He smiled, picking up his coffee cup. "Yes, I suppose that is what I mean."

"At home?"

"I didn't know the home life, nor should I tell you if I did." He was suddenly serious.

"Of course not." He hadn't meant to imply as much as he had. Perhaps, too, the problem was in the money, not in the wife.

"Was Stedman broke when he married Mrs. Larch?"

"Not absolutely. I can tell you that—especially since he is legally dead. A few thousand saved—two or three—but no real assets to speak of."

"So he might have been subservient?"

"I can't answer that." This time his face showed nothing. A good lawyer's face, or a poker player's. He motioned to the waitress for more coffee and lighted a cigarette. The restaurant was nearly empty, and we were no longer on the original subject, yet he made no effort to leave. He would see the interview to an ordinary finish.

"Why do you think a woman of her position would marry Stedman, someone with no connections?"

"You want me to talk about her." He hesitated. "Well, to be honest, I don't know. He was handsome, as I recall, and charming. I don't know about his education. Perhaps she was distressed. I no more know the reasons than I know why your father never remarried."

I nodded. Perhaps these general reasons were the cause. It may have flattered her to be attractive to a younger man. It might even be true that she wouldn't be able to say why now—because she hated him as much as she may have cared for him.

"What's it like to be a private detective, David?"

"Private. My life and my time are often my own."

"Now, no offense intended"—he smiled—"but do you ever feel like a voyeur?" He meant to offend, but I ignored him and treated his comment as a joke.

"I've never been a voyeur, so I can't speak in direct comparison. No. In relation to my clients no more than as an attorney. It's a minor way of achieving truth—not only what we are, but why. And if you'll pardon me, now it is more honest for me than the law."

"Perhaps. I see your point." I knew he did and didn't give a damn. "But you could make more as a lawyer with your father. You'd be his partner. What do you make?"

"When I work, $150 to $200 a day, plus expenses."

"Let's see, how old are you?"

"Thirty-four."

"With that much time and experience you could make about $75 an hour in law." Then he shrugged. "But it's your choice."

"I have enough." He knew I did, too. He wanted to needle me, and the only reason I could see was that my questions annoyed him after all; he had opened a crack into his family.

"I don't ordinarily have dessert. Do you care for any?"

I said no. He motioned to the waitress, insisted on paying, then waited until she left.

"I expect you to treat the Larches with respect, David. Especially Mrs. Larch." He put his hand to his chin and eyed me directly as if practicing a courtroom technique that he never needed.

"I do that with all my clients."

"Certainly. Knowing your father, I wouldn't expect less of you. But they are important people—I cannot emphasize how important—and she has suffered enough over this." He stressed his vague *this*. "It took great courage for her to go on when her husband left." There was almost a tremor in his voice.

"I understand you, Mr. Bolen."

"I hope so. I can tell you if I had had any idea what was in that letter, then that skeleton would still be in the ground. And you would be out of a job."

No, I thought, I'd be in Chicago, probably making more and doing less for it.

"Don't make me put you out of a job." I knew he could. He was the second man to threaten my job.

He hadn't taken his eyes from me, and his face was stern. He hoped by admonishment to protect his client. Perhaps he had confided more than he wished he had. I had the feeling it would not be a troublesome point of conscience for him. Suddenly he smiled with a slight shake of the head, as though I were a wayward but forgiven child.

"It's been a pleasure to see you again, David. Must be fifteen years now. I appreciate your letting me know what was happening."

He stood and I followed him out. When we had picked up our coats and were standing in the damp, he repeated his offer of help, adding that he would be glad to hear of further developments. After he left I went back into the restaurant to make some phone calls.

My father wasn't in his office, but I left a message with his secretary that I would like to see him if he could arrange the time. I told her she could give my answering service the message. Then I started looking through the directory for Roscoes. On my fourth call a woman paused when I asked if this was Dwight Roscoe's family. Then she asked in a tremulous voice who I was.

I gave her my name and told her why I wanted to see her. After what were obviously anxious seconds for her, she told me to come over at three-thirty.

When I hung up I gave Bob Stedman a call. He wasn't in and wasn't expected soon. I decided to go ahead and retrieve the letter from my safety deposit box and to call him again later. It was time to give Carlson the letter. I smiled. By evening I would have given myself a twenty-four-hour lead, and Carlson would be still angrier.

8

Deciding it would be easier to walk than to find a parking place, I splashed through four blocks of slush to the bank. It was nearly empty; the television eyes in the corners looked down on its almost abandoned world inhabited by two tellers, a guard, a sixty-year-old woman in a far too youthful black leather coat, and me. I went to the vault, retrieved the letter and slogged back to West 3rd Street.

I drove to the near west side, not glamorous but industrious. A catch basin near the end of the street was clogged, and black water, covered with gray chunks of ice and snow and edged by foam, backed across the street. The water washed up into the underside of the car, its wake lapping at the curbs and over the devil strip. The house I was looking for was an old white frame structure with a broad front porch and probably four bedrooms in its square dimensions. The garage at the end of the driveway still had the swinging, windowed doors, locked closed by a sliding vertical bolt rammed into the driveway. Snow had drifted slightly against the door.

The woman who answered the door in an unbelted housedress was between fifty and sixty. I couldn't be certain because her skin had collapsed into numerous wrinkles over her thin face, just as the dress fell in folds over her body.

"Miss Roscoe? I'm David Stuart."

"Of course. Won't you come in?"

She stepped back, and I walked into the past, a house that smelled old. A combination of mustiness and cooking odors. The furniture was old-fashioned, except for a couch of traditional square design. In the next room, through an arch partially closed by its sliding doors, I could hear a television. Its light flickered in the darkness.

"Won't you sit down? I'm sorry about the noise from the television, but Mother likes to have it on, and she can't hear very well. We made a bedroom for her down here so she would be near the kitchen and could see her friends when they come."

Miss Roscoe had the tired, high-pitched voice that went with years of sickroom attendance and the recluse's desire to talk about life.

"What's wrong with your mother?"

"A cerebrovascular accident." She waited to be certain I had understood. "She doesn't remember things very well now, not the way she used to. It's very sad. She used to be able to read a newspaper and tell you everything in it."

"Did she have the stroke recently?"

"Oh, no." She smiled faintly, wistfully, when she heard the harsh layman's term. "It was five years ago, the last one. She's eighty-three. The doctor says it's a miracle she's alive, but then I take good care of her."

"I'm sure you do." I smiled and felt the strain in my face.

"She had her first accident when she was seventy."

"Before your brother disappeared?"

"Yes. She still asks for him." She motioned to me with her left hand to move closer. "You know, she can't keep the experiences straight. Sometimes she thinks I'm just a little girl. I don't mind. How can I?"

I could only think she was right, and I added to myself—what difference would it make?

She went on, heedless that I hadn't given an answer, not really expecting one. "You said on the phone that you wanted to ask me about my brother."

"If you don't mind."

"It's very painful; Dwight and I were always close. We took

care of each other and our parents." She paused, her hands cupped over her knees as she leaned forward. "He was a policeman until my father fell and broke his hip. He went fast—pneumonia—but there were bills, so many bills."

She spoke a catalogue of pain that was ugly in its repetition, and not yet over, because her brother was still missing.

"That was when he became a detective. He thought he could make more money, even though he said he knew ways to stay on the force and make more. Dwight was too honest to do that. Always a model for me, even though I was three years older. He has to be dead." The tone was shocking to hear, for she moved to her conclusion without changing the lilt of reminiscence.

"Why do you think he has to be dead?"

"Because he'd never desert us. He worked too hard and cared too much." Now she became emphatic. "No. He has to be dead."

"He was working for a family named Larch when he disappeared."

"I remember. They are rich people. They paid him two weeks in advance. He gave me that money and used the later fees to pay his expenses." She rushed through her next thought before slowing her recitation. "He worked hard on that for six months. I couldn't forget that, not the last thing he did. He never said where he was going the time he didn't come back, but it was out of the city. You know what I did with that money he gave me? Used it to try to find him. But I didn't know how to do that, so I hired a detective, but he didn't find Dwight. Strange, isn't it . . . at least I always thought so . . . how a detective's sister would not know how to hire a detective." She did not look amused by the irony she described.

"What was his name?"

"The detective? Phil Buckman."

"Did he learn anything?"

"No." She shrugged her shoulders, and the wrinkles in her face became pained. "I might as well have done all the looking. But that's all over."

The television blared a commercial for furniture polish, to

the tune of a once-popular song. The light flickered brightly.

"How do you get along now?"

"Dribs and drabs." She smiled gratefully at the question. "Social security and a small pension. We were paid Dwight's insurance money two years ago. I had to file that he was dead."

"Did Dwight ever tell you anything about the case?"

"No, no facts. He was very reliable. He kept his customers' secrets. Only I know he thought it was big. I think he knew something when he left here. I can still see him in the kitchen, telling me the case might be worth more than he'd ever dreamed."

"Did he explain to you what he meant?"

"I told you he could keep secrets."

"If you should think of anything, call me."

"Of course. I'd like to know what happened to Dwight."

I couldn't tell her we might never know and that I hadn't been hired to find him. Dwight Roscoe was simply a piece in a larger design. "Can I use your phone book?"

She brought it to me from an old mahogany combination phone stand and chair and I found a Phil Buckman. He wasn't listed under detectives, but I still thought it was better to drive over than to call.

"How did you happen to choose Buckman to look for your brother?" I walked back with her as she replaced the directory.

"He was nearby, so I wouldn't be away from the house for long. I didn't like to leave Mother. Dwight had never told me about other detectives, so I had no way of knowing who was good or bad." She said the last words slowly. "Was I wrong?"

"No. You had as good a reason for your choice as anyone."

I thanked her and had started down the steps when she called to stop me.

"Mr. Stuart, I just happened to think, I gave Dwight's file to Mr. Buckman—because I thought it might help him to find my brother."

"I'll ask to see it."

She nodded and stepped back inside without speaking.

Buckman was now superintendent of a fifty-year-old apartment building, living in a basement apartment at the dimly lighted bottom of a half flight of dirty steps whose treads were covered with worn brown rubber. There was no answer to my first rap of the knocker. I made the metallic click three more times, then waited. After a few seconds a heavy shuffling sound came from the other side of the door. The knocker clattered again as the door opened.

"Mr. Buckman?"

He nodded. I could smell the results of his occupational hazard on his breath. Buckman was just under six feet, and if he had ever been in shape, he no longer was. His red and yellow cotton flannel shirt was partly untucked; the right side hung from the roll that protruded above his belt, which turned down the waistband of his trousers. A white-socked toe protruded through the worn end of a red corduroy slipper. It was obvious from a crease on his left cheek that I'd awakened him.

"My name is Stuart. I'm a private detective and I'm working on a case that involves someone you once worked for. I understand you were once a detective."

As soon as I started to speak, he tried to give me the eye by cocking his head and letting his jaw go slack, something he had probably seen on television. But as soon as I referred to his previous occupation his face relaxed into a foolish grin that let the flesh of his cheeks puff out.

"Come on in, Mr. . . . what did you say your name was?"

"Stuart."

"Come on in. I like to talk over old times. There's nobody around here believes an old bag like me once did that."

The room had been furnished twenty years before with one stop at a used-furniture store. It had been cleaned as recently. Two chairs and a couch, much the worse for wear, were upholstered in a green fabric that had taken on a gray cast, except where spotted, and had lost its nap. A couple of tables were cheap colonial imitation maple. He turned on a floor lamp at one end of the couch; then, with greater coordination than I assumed him capable of, he stooped and in a single movement picked a newspaper from the floor and dropped it over a couple of girlie magazines on the coffee table in front of me.

"Would you like a beer?"

"Not just now. I had a late lunch today."

"I think I'll have one, if it's okay with you. I get kinda thirsty this time of day."

"Go on. I'll wait here."

He hustled out, and no sooner did a bottle cap snap than he returned, set the bottle on the table, pulled up the matching armchair, took a large glass ashtray from the one end table and set it before him, then sat back in his chair. Only then did he slow to a pace more suited to his bulk.

"Now then, do you care for a cigar? I've only got one in my pocket, but there's a whole box full over there." He gestured behind him.

"No, thanks. You go ahead."

"You sure?"

"Yes."

"Now then," as he exhaled, making a screen for himself, "which of my former customers is you concerned for?"

"Dwight Roscoe."

"Yeah, I remember. The mousy sister. Yeah. Well, I never found him."

"Nothing?"

"Not him. I'd have to look him up—it's hard to remember that far back. How long ago was that?" He sucked at the bottle, taking down half its contents, returning a long rolling belch.

"Ten years."

He eyed the bottle approvingly. "Beer in a can don't taste the same. I don't care what anybody says. Ten years. Now I'm surprised I remember the sister. 'Cept that must have been nearly my last case. Took away my license. Claimed I was extorting, taking bribes." He put on a morose look, one that wasn't very different from the way he had looked at me by the door, except that he wasn't looking at me. Again he sucked on the bottle, but only for a couple of swallows. Then he noticed the cigar in his right hand and created another cloud. I leaned back and waited. He'd get to the point when he wanted to.

"Hell, they never busted me. That's what the kids say on TV now—busted. Just took my license. But what the hell! I got this job right afterwards, and I don't have to bust my ass running all around, not knowing what I'm doing. You don't look like life is too bad for you, not in those threads. That sister can't be paying you."

"I get by okay."

"Yeah. But then so do I. Got a roof, TV, my beer and cigars. My only problems are faucets and toilets. Or maybe a snowstorm like last night's. That was a pain in the ass."

"Yeah, it would be. But the job doesn't sound bad."

"That's right." He laughed, sucked the remaining beer out, and dropped the bottle to the floor by his chair. The bottle stood. "Now, you wanted to know about Roscoe. He was a go-getter. Had to be, working for those people he did." Buckman's memory was better than he would admit.

"He had a family to take care of."

"That sister?" He pointed a finger at me. "And you don't." He tapped the cigar on the ashtray. "Let me get that file."

He walked to a small dining area off the living room, where the only contents were a painted table, two unmatched chairs and a two-drawer file. Everything, including one chair, was littered—dishes, clothes, newspapers. I wondered how long it took him to fix a faucet.

"That cigar stinks, don't it?" He'd laid it on the edge of the cabinet as he used both hands to go through the first and then the second drawer.

"It's fragrant."

"That's a nice way to say it stinks." He turned and grinned widely at me. The space for a left upper incisor was now visible. He took out a folder and slammed the drawer, knocking the cigar off between the cabinet and the wall. Again he was a burst of unexpected energy. Dropping the folder, he shoved the cabinet aside, picked up the cigar and stomped on the floor. He chuckled as he moved the file back.

"Wouldn't do for me to burn the place down, would it?" He laughed outright. I had to laugh and shake my head.

"Here. This is a neat folder. That's because Roscoe did most of it. The couple of pages on top are mine."

The top pages were three-ringed notebook paper. Often the

writing wasn't even on the lines and was illegible. In contrast, Roscoe kept a carefully written page.

"I read through these files every now and then. Most of them are dull, cheap divorces. Roscoe's was the only interesting case, a missing person. But they're as good as TV—sometimes. Hell, I should've stayed a shoe salesman. That was what I did the longest, after I quit school. But I didn't stick with it. I never stuck to anything—not even my wife—until I got this job. And I'm doing good to stay so long." He laughed again, but this time the laughter was forced. "You trying to read those now? Okay, I'll leave you alone for a while."

He lifted himself heavily from his chair and went to the kitchen. I heard another bottle opened; then he started walking farther away; and next he was urinating, the sound coming through an open door.

Roscoe didn't use names or even initials, only numbers and letters, which didn't clarify matters. It was immediately clear that Roscoe was on to something more than Stedman's disappearance. Robbery was the felony referred to; but, sitting there on the broken springs of Buckman's couch, nothing went together. Roscoe hadn't written much into his file; the small, neat handwriting was meaningless unless the code and abbreviations were broken.

Buckman's return was preceded by another belch. The beer was in his right hand.

"Did you find what you wanted?"

"I'm not sure. Could I take this?"

"Well . . ."

"I'll pay you for it, as an informant."

"Hundred dollars."

"I don't know if it's worth a thing I can't find on my own. Twenty."

"Seventy-five. You're working for some rich bastard instead of that Roscoe woman."

"Twenty's all I'll spring."

"Sold." He grinned. "Twenty's cheap when I figure it's the only good-looking file I got."

"So sell your beauty. What are the others worth?"

"You're right. Nothing." He stuck out his lower lip. "Besides, it's Roscoe's."

I gave him the money. He folded it and pushed it down in his shirt pocket.

"Can't I get you a beer now?"

"No. I've got to get going. But maybe you could tell me if you ever made anything of this file."

"Sure can." Again he sucked at the bottle, pleased to give advice. "Roscoe was looking for somebody involved in an armed robbery."

"Not a bad memory, after ten years."

He blushed, surprising me as much as himself. "Well, I told you I read the files every once in a while. And that was the best one," he repeated.

"No doubt it was."

"It's the only serious case I ever saw."

"Anything else?"

"Naw." He shook his head in a wide arc. "I was never any good at that business. Nobody in his right mind would give me a case like that one." He laughed and shook his head again. "You think that sister's crazy?"

I used his phone to call the answering service. My father had left a message to come to his house at seven. I decided to call Bob Stedman from a drugstore.

9

Bob wasn't home. The maid who answered didn't know where he was or when he would return. I gave my name and said I would call back. For now there was no reason to puzzle over his absence.

It was pointless to go home, so I drove out Carnegie, up Cedar Hill to Fairmount, then across to Shaker Boulevard. The house I grew up in was a couple of blocks off the boulevard, about a mile beyond the square. The street was filled with big houses that took up their lots. Massive, mostly older, expensive, but not the first in the city. For twenty-two years, I thought as I drove up the drive, this was home; comfortable, to most it would have been luxury. I parked in back by the garage he didn't use. The driveway had been plowed, the snow pushed into a pile beside my car; some of it was across the street. On the lawn the snow lay heavy and compact. Under the oak tree that once held a swing for me the snow was pockmarked by dripping water. Beyond the tree was the rose garden—three to four dozen mounds of carefully hilled roses—that looked like some primitive graveyard where the dead had been treated to courteous, yet now unfathomable ceremony. In a way, my father's own way, that was the case. The garden had been my mother's, and he kept it. First he kept it as a trust to their lives; then it was his, and he added to it, renewing and planting. In the years since I left home I could count on one hand the number of times I had seen him in the summer evenings when he wasn't working on the roses. They were work for him because he was a perfectionist, but he never would have seen them as such, or his labor as more than diversion.

I walked around to the front of the house. Mrs. Barnes, an ageless black woman who might have been fifty but was probably sixty-five, opened the door before I rang the bell. She had worked for my mother and stayed on when she died. About five years earlier her husband had died, and she had moved into the maid's room that had never before in my life been occupied. She was slight—a testimony to her view that work never hurt anyone.

"Hello, David. I was in the kitchen and saw you park your car. Your father called to say you would be here for dinner."

"How are you, Mrs. Barnes?" We had that way of addressing each other that reached into the past. I was formally a child to her and she formally an adult I had been told to listen to. We weren't cold or distant; we simply knew each other on those terms.

"Fine, just fine. Give me your coat."

"I thought I would find you here." I laid the folder on a table and took off my coat.

"Where else would I be?" She smiled as though I were still a child. "Did you come for dinner or to make your father busier?"

"That's my work. I thought I could use his library while I waited."

"You are early. But don't you trouble him."

"I was downtown and decided it would be pointless to go to my place when you would be here."

"Well, you go on and do your work. I'll keep busy in the kitchen till Mr. Stuart comes home." She hung up my coat and went back through the center hall to the kitchen without speaking again.

I went to my right into the library. The desk was off the back wall, facing the door—cleared except for a desk set and reading lamp. The walls were lined with books on every subject but primarily on history and anthropology. There was a brown leather easy chair in one corner, a floor lamp beside it. The only object in the room that was different was a gun case by the door. Through its glass doors were visible two iron bars, padlocked, across a bolt action .22, an old Winchester .30-.30, two twenty-gauge shotguns and one twelve-gauge shotgun. Each gun had a lock on its trigger. I pulled on the handle. The case was locked. I put the folder on the desk and sat down. The light seemed widely diffused in the dusky late-afternoon light that filled the room. It lacked the sharpness of a light in a darkened room.

The .22 was the first gun I ever fired. He bought it for me when I was thirteen, almost a year and a half after my mother died in an automobile accident. He had hunted off and on ever since I could remember; the Winchester was his. Though he never said so, I knew the gun was to give us an excuse to spend some time together. For twelve years, as I grew up, he'd worked at a career. I understood his work was necessary, or so I was told, and had accepted. Not for money—my mother as an only child had inherited a considerable income from her grandfather—but for purpose. My mother seemed to believe in the same purpose; at least in my memory she never demurred. I don't believe she did in reality, either, for that wasn't her family's way. She had been to Connecticut to visit them when she died. Her inheritance, or most of it, came to me, but by then, when he was thirty-eight, the money didn't matter to my father. He had found a purpose in the Depression in public service, and it stood him well after the war, when the people he worked for were wealthy—or at least some were. He was independent of my mother's family's money by then. Whether he was guilty or made himself free, after her death we spent our first time together. Hunting was the one activity he'd had before, so now he included me. He taught me to shoot; with the rifle he was expert. Even the Winchester would be precise for him.

He never bought me a heavier rifle. When I was fifteen we went deer hunting in Pennsylvania for the second time. The year before, he had shown me how to follow and lead a moving target, but he did the killing with the .30-.30. The second year when we were out he gave me his rifle. That small circle, behind and below the shoulder, moved up and down faster and faster forward until as I squeezed off that first shot it seemed a mechanical extension of the rifle, my mind unable to separate subject and object, need from fear. Then the white tail pitched forward, and I'd separated the deer from the rifle and from me. All I recall before standing over a still panting but clearly dying buck was my father's hand on my shoulder and his voice reassuring. When we saw that the animal was still alive, he took the rifle from me, pulled the lever down again, put the butt on his shoulder and shot the deer in the head. We never took trophies; we never even took the meat. My father always stopped at an orphanage on the way home with the animal we had. The first year we had gone hunting, when he had killed a buck with one shot, I remembered the blood in the hair. My deer fell on its wound, and only when we rolled it over was I shocked at what I'd done. I wasn't sick, but there was a complete consciousness of individual vulnerability, a feeling I had not known even when I learned that my mother was dead.

For the moment I said nothing. In fact, I didn't say a dozen words until we left the carcass in the stainless steel and white porcelain orphanage kitchen. But from that moment in the woods when I saw the wound I had made, I pondered why my father had continued to hunt, to teach me to shoot, to let me kill, after my mother died. I never had an answer; I was afraid to ask him. I must have felt intuitively that the subject was too personal for me to intrude. Though I never knew, I wondered if it was the vulnerability he wanted me to know and to accept. We didn't go deer hunting again. The next year he bought the twenty-gauge shotguns—to try something new, he'd said. Upland hunting—small birds. He borrowed a good friend's dog. We didn't shoot anything. Neither of us. The next year, the year before college, we took the shotguns, but at the last minute we left them in the car and only walked. Neither of us cared any more about the hunt and kill, for we knew the lesson.

I doubted if there was a single cartridge or shell in the house, but I was sure he cleaned the guns every year, an act of responsibility. He learned with shock that I'd bought the .38 revolver and thought of giving up the law practice; he was guilty—at least that was how I first read his face. But it was, by then, the twin lessons of responsibility and vulnerability I had learned. Subject and object could be separated, but not without a vision of accountability imprinted in bloodied fur. So the gun was not the greatest shock for him, just as those hunting trips were not responsible for my hunting men. I had seen, finally, in those trips, a moral responsibility that was ultimate and that was necessary truth. Over ten years later I knew there was such a thing as truth and final cause, and the memory of the day I killed the deer was my image that one could know—only that with men accountability was harder to explain. Others could reach, had reached, the conclusion without seeing the mechanical union of subject and object to cause and effect in a breathless dying animal. I think I would have, but I'll never know.

I turned my head from the glass door with its double image, a transparency which allowed me to see the guns and opaque reflection of light, to the manila folder before me. Roscoe protected his client and his case. No one reading his single handwritten page could tell who the persons were, unless he had the advantage of knowing the names of the principal persons. There were no copies of the letters he had sent Mrs. Larch. The figures in the left-hand margin were an immediate but temporary problem. The numbers were consecutive, with one exception, but they began at 100. Then I knew that he dated everything from the beginning of the year.

April 10, 1967.

- 100   A last seen at 11:14
- 101   C reported missing by B
- 103   A reported missing
- 104   Hired. SECRET. B is helpful—too much?
- 105   Check employment records of A and C. No contacts.
- 109   Possible ID of C at AA. Sometime 102 or 103 P.M.
- 119   Bos. A was here alone. No record of C.
- 129   B dead. Searched house. D worked for B; was contact for job.
-   65   S - L robbery. A was witness. Did A deal with D?
- 170   Tell employer to stop search.

171 Told to return Bos.
172 Check C's University placement record. 1-6. Exp 3.
173 Alb. - N.A.
175 Told to negotiate.

So Roscoe's record ended on June 24, 1967. I read it through again and again, filling in abbreviations and letters, trying to come up with a workable explanation of the notes. The one fact that required no deciphering, the robbery, was of a savings and loan on March 7. That would be easy to check. His employer had to be Bolen, working for the Larches. There was no hope that he would help me, but I could figure out some more parts before I saw the Larches. If A was Stedman, then C was Ellen Penn. They were the ones missing. B was Penn, who died in a plane crash in Chicago. I couldn't identify D, or what his job was, except that it might be the robbery. I figured out how Roscoe wound up in Bos. Boston, probably. After starting on Ellen Penn's trail, he wound up on Stedman's. Ten days had passed and he'd made no entry. I wondered if it was because of innate caution or real distrust, or possibly carelessness. Damn. A ten-year-old record left by a man who was probably dead.

I looked at the last entries. Ellen Penn's college records gave some clue that led Roscoe to—Alabama, Albany, Albuquerque? I would assume C was Ellen and try to get a lead from 173. And who requested the negotiation, and what was it for?

Roscoe kept most of the information in his head. Apparently this list was in the order he learned his facts, which explained the one upset in chronology. The only explanation that he would write any information down was that he recorded only what he forwarded. That way, if Bolen or any other intermediary wasn't straight, he had his own file. But what Bolen didn't need to know, what was handwritten, had been withheld in Roscoe's head. I could guess the reason for the rest of the night, but wouldn't come any closer. Buckman's scribbling was useless, so I closed the folder over Roscoe's single sheet, having decided to visit the library the next morning and then to find out what Ellen Penn's alma mater was.

I took the folder back to the front hall and laid it on the table again. Then I wandered back to the kitchen.

"What's for dinner, Mrs. Barnes?"

"Chicken cacciatora." She was thin lipped, seriously stirring a large pot.

"You're too tense."

"You think this is a pot of beans that cooks itself?"

"No. Black-eyed peas."

"You rascal." She smiled. "It's a good thing I've known you since you were little."

"Then tell me what's after you, before I sue you for abridging my civil rights."

"What right are you deprived of?" She smiled in spite of herself, playing the part opposite me.

"Why, my right to know that your grim face won't spoil that chicken cacciatora. I didn't come over here for heartburn."

"Well, you won't get it, if you'll leave me alone. And if you behave yourself while you're here." She was smiling, but her voice had a cool edge.

"So, you suspect ulterior motives."

"I don't want you to disturb your father."

"Any particular reason?"

"He's never gotten over your quitting."

"Yes, he has."

"No."

"But that's not all of it."

"He's been working hard lately. Don't you upset him."

"Okay."

"Don't you get out that work you brought."

"I don't think I'll need to."

"Don't." Her lips were a line, darker than her light brown skin. She folded her wiry arms across her chest as she said the word.

"All right." I smiled, and she seemed to accept me again, for she turned back to her pot, taking the spoon in her right hand.

I walked to the sink, took a glass and a bottle of Scotch from the cabinet to the right, poured a drink, and left her working. I went back to the living room, turned on the lights and started through the latest issue of *Newsweek*. About a half hour later, as I finished my drink, I heard my father come in the back door. He said a few words to Mrs. Barnes, then came into the front hall. He'd unbuttoned his topcoat. If he was tired I didn't see it. He was as straight as I remembered him from our last meeting at Christmas, and his face and white hair shone above his black coat and dark blue glen-plaid suit. When we shook hands he used both hands.

"Dave, you treat me as though I were an adversary. Where have you been?"

"I was away. Went south for a week or so. I only got back a few days ago."

"I missed you at New Year's. So did your aunt and uncle."

"Sorry to be away. It was the opportunity, and I needed a break, to get away." I felt apologetic.

"I know what you mean. I understand." He patted my shoulder. "Let me hang up my coat, and I'll get us a drink."

"I've got a glass in the living room." I retrieved it and came back to the hall as he put his coat away.

He saw the folder on the table as he closed the closet door. "That yours?"

I nodded.

"Did you have something for me to look over?"

"No. I picked that up after I called you, and rather than take it home, I've been looking it over in your study."

His face was blank for a moment, as though let down. He wanted to do something with me. Then he let a smile return, and nodded. "Okay, let's get that drink."

I felt edgy. I had come on purpose, and he had to know that. I wanted him to ask me why, yet I had just let an opportunity slip away. Perhaps I didn't want to hurt him by appearing to want only business advice and not a father's help.

While he poured two Scotches we talked of the weather, the roads, the day in general, almost as Bolen and I had, which made me feel bad. We went back to the living room. He asked about my trip, shaking his head that anyone would go there in winter. Then, like Mary, he asked about Chris.

"You still see her?"

"Yes. But not for a month."

"You going to marry her?" He put his glass on an end table. We sat on facing couches that were at right angles to the fireplace. I could see he was serious, and I suspected that my answer wouldn't please him or satisfy him.

"I don't know. We've only talked of it in the most general way. We both know it would be a marriage with separations in it."

"That's not the way your mother and I were. But you and Karen . . . " He simply stopped. "It's hard for me to understand."

"I know. Is that why you never remarried?"

He raised his eyebrows, either in puzzlement or as a reflex indicating thought. "At first. That's a long time ago. Why did you ask?"

"The topic was marriage, not just me."

He nodded. "I opened the can of worms—that's not an encouraging metaphor." He laughed softly, almost to himself, then took a drink. "Then you were there. Almost for the first time, for me. You knew that, too, didn't you?"

"Yes, but only at that time. There was a vacuum we each rushed in to fill."

"After you went to college, there was the firm." He shrugged. "Way leads on to way."

"Do you think of her now?"

He slumped back, his right index finger running around the rim of his glass.

"I'm sorry, that's not my business."

"Why not?" He paused and looked out a window at the darkness. "After twenty-three years? Sometimes. I'm not a sentimental idiot. But, yes, perhaps that was why . . . all the time. But you know, don't you? It's hard going on. And I had you. When Karen died, you were alone. Is she why you don't marry Chris? Now I apologize. Only . . . well . . . ."

"Only we both know the feeling."

He nodded.

Karen was murdered four years before in the hospital parking lot. Mrs. Heller's labor was long, almost fifteen hours, so

Karen finally left the hospital after three in the morning. Someone, never found, stole her purse after stabbing her twice. It was shortly after six when Steve Horning from the D.A.'s office woke me and told me. He came because we had worked together for two years and were still friends, and he didn't want a stranger to take me to the coroner's office. He stayed with me that morning, an act that breeds indebtedness, strangely, on both sides.

After he finally got out the terrible reason for his visit, I felt my throat constrict. Even though I knew when I saw him in our door. All I remember was the feeling in my throat and my head moving. I know I shook my head, but I never knew why. Whether in denial or pain or anger or sickness. But she was dead, and nothing I could think or say would deny my knowledge of what her pallor meant when I looked down on her face. I had worked too long in criminal prosecution to be shocked by death, but not so long that Karen's face could not cause me to cry.

We were the same age, were married for five and a half years; and I put her through her last year of medical school after I finished law school. She was bright and intense, more so than I, and I felt gratitude that she loved me. I shared her with all her mothers and babies, for she did love them in a collective maternal way. Over some she agonized as only someone untainted by the world could. As yet I was unable to think of Karen with ease; probably I never will. Once she was all I ever needed, and she no longer existed. Though what they did was dissimilar, she and Chris were basically similar. Perhaps I was afraid of repetition. I know I found it difficult to believe how fortunate I was in the two women I had loved.

I did not become a detective because Karen's murder was unsolved. I had quit my father's office the year before, after we had discussed the step for months. I needed a value which the law, the courts, practice, the rules of evidence, and a dozen other things did not provide. Karen sympathized and accepted; approval was never a question. And it was tough for a while to watch her go off to give life a start. Not that her work was all pleasure. After all, some children are deformed, some never even breathe; and those were always painful times for Karen. But her work was joyful. At first I had no work; then a couple of friends sent me work. My father never did, whether from hurt or fear. But his contacts helped, as did mine through the D.A.'s office, and the fact that communications were privileged finally helped the most, because no matter what people had to spill out, they were afraid. But the hard part was to continue to convince myself that to know the truth was more important than any legal form of retribution.

He had looked down for several minutes, lost in himself, before he asked, "Are you still serious in what you do?"

"Of course. Doesn't it show?"

"Not the way it did that day you quit."

"No, it's not the same. But I had to be serious then, to tell you. That was the hardest decision I ever made. There was no way I could make it and not hurt you."

"No." He shook his head. "Are you glad you changed?"

"Not to have left you, but to have changed."

"The two are inseparable for me."

"It's not a matter of love me, love my dog. I'm sorry for that."

"That's all right, but your comparison is false. Anyway, I only wanted you to be happy . . . and secure."

"I am. You know I don't have to worry about money."

"That's not all I meant. What about happy? Are you?"

"It's not all it seemed to me it would be, but I'm still glad I'm doing it."

"Why? Can I go over that again with you? Maybe it's my age, maybe the day. Can I?"

"Sure."

"You gave up a reputable profession where you had a clear future, for a disreputable job that could get you killed."

"That's TV."

"Maybe the killing is, but you know as well as I do that you moved down the ladder. Like you didn't want the risks in law."

"It's my image that disturbs you."

He nodded. "Partly. Most cops would be happy to have a law degree, to get out of the line of fire."

"Maybe. I don't know."

"Was it me?"

"No. I told you before."

"You're still the idealist—wanting moral certainty."

"Probably." I took a long drink. "It wasn't you. Until Chris, you and Karen were the only persons I respected." I paused; his eyes were on me. "While I was in the study I saw the gun rack. Those years came back for me. I'm glad I had them with you."

"I am, too." Then, almost afraid of feeling, he sounded like an attorney: "Now, as to why you're here . . ."

"There's no reason."

"It doesn't do much for an idealist to lie. I had a call from Alec Bolen today."

Mrs. Barnes came in to tell us dinner was ready, and despite her earlier injunction, as we ate I told him about Roscoe's file—the single enigmatic page. The talk rambled without adding to what I knew to do. Only after dinner did I ask about Bolen's deal.

We sat at the table, both in armchairs; he at the end where French windows opened onto a terrace, I opposite.

"You think either Stedman or Penn was involved in a robbery?"

"I don't know. Obviously Roscoe knew something. I'll have to dig into some old newspapers."

"Want a brandy?"

"No, not tonight."

"Courvoisier—you sure you won't have some?" He stood up, went to the sideboard and took a bottle from behind the right-hand cabinet door. The cognac snifters were behind the liquor. He poured some, then set both bottle and glass on the table. "You sure?" He tipped the top of the bottle. When I nodded he sat down.

"What did Bolen tell you when he called?"

"That you were working on that sensational murder, for Stedman's son. That you were interested in the business and that he referred you to me on that matter."

"Well, he was open."

"I wouldn't have expected less."

"No." I smiled. "You wouldn't. Your trust is one of the things I like best about you. It's a quality I never learned from you."

"Believing in friends?" He picked up the snifter but only held it.

"You and he aren't that close."

"No, you're right. And I wasn't trying to impress you or fool myself. Colleague is the word I should have used."

"It doesn't matter. The fact is I came to ask you not because you're my father, but because I can believe you."

"But not Bolen?" His tone was curious, genuinely unbelieving, but patient.

"I take little at face value, and even then I've gone wrong."

"At the risk of sounding sententious, I believe in trust."

"I want to, but I've found that too many people don't, and I have to protect myself. Did he say you were free to tell me about the deal?"

"Yes. What do you need to know?"

"You were made absentee trustee?" I asked.

"For Stedman's half of the partnership. You know the law requires a seven-year period before the absentee's death is presumed and the estate collectible. I was able to argue that the sale was necessary to Bob Stedman, despite his mother's wealth. She wanted to be rid of the business as a connection to her husband."

"The price offered was fair?"

"Too much so, which helped. In retrospect I can see that it was a good investment, but Bob Stedman was only a child then."

"Did you have the accounts audited? Was the inventory checked?"

He laughed. "Of course." He took his first sip of brandy.

"Was everything in order?"

He nodded and swallowed. "What are you going to do?"

"If I can . . . find out what Roscoe learned. If I'm right about what he found, would you have pushed to settle the estate?"

"But you're not really sure."

"No. But do you think the search was adequate?"

"Perhaps not. I had to go on the evidence Bolen gave me. What he had from Roscoe. And I had to consider my client."

"Bob?" I asked.

"He was a child. Mrs. Larch." He raised the snifter again, inhaled, then took some brandy on his tongue. "That's the very type of situation which bothered you—with its absence of certainty."

"Possibly. Now it is. But then I would also have accepted the detective's report and Bolen's word."

"What about protecting and serving your client?"

"I do what I can to protect. But I have a limit. I told Bob I would turn his father in if he was alive and was guilty."

"So you still serve the law." He smiled with what I thought was relief as he made his point.

"In part. Yes, you have me there. Only it doesn't stop there. I believe in punishment, but I can live without it. Knowing I've done the most I can to get at reality is what I want, is where I get satisfaction."

"You do like your work . . . what you said earlier was true."

"You can trust me." I smiled at my assertion. "I said most of the time."

"Is homicide the kind of case you usually take?"

"No. Missing persons."

"Who's missing?"

"Paul Stedman."

"Who is legally dead."

"But perhaps not actually."

"And that's why you do what you do."

"Yes, because nearly always there's a difference between assumption and reality."

He was quiet for several minutes, finishing his brandy.

"Don't take chances, Dave. I like you; you're what I have . . . and that's important to me. Why do you think I bother to keep those guns? I'll never go hunting again. I've built a solid reputation, but I'm very alone. I'm not telling you this for pity, but because I need to talk to you."

"I understand."

"It hurt me when you left the firm. As much as it pleased me when you left the prosecutor to join me. And I may never fully understand or appreciate what you say you need to do. But I want to. You ought to marry Chris; then you'd have a reason to be careful. And only one of us would be alone."

"That's no reason to get married."

He grinned. "It's better than many."

An hour or so later I left. We went to the back door. When he turned on the outside light, the mounds that were the rose bushes formed patterns of intense white snow and dark shadows intermingled, cutting across each other with a crisp exactness they didn't have in the gray daylight.

I drove by Chris's, stopping in front of the driveway to see the garage. But there were no lights on the second floor. I was disappointed.

10

At nine the next morning I was at the library. *The Plain Dealer* for the morning of March 7, 1967 was ugly reading. The front page was filled with the news of a brutal savings and loan robbery. Three armored-car guards were slain outright and three-quarters of a million dollars stolen. The men were shot without warning by two men apparently carrying sawed-off shotguns and a third with a pistol. Coming from three sides and firing from close range, and perhaps from under their coats, the killers gave their victims, who held drawn revolvers, no chance. They took the truck, dropping it by a warehouse several blocks away but on the truck's normal route. The crime was as calculated as it was savage and sick. Accompanying articles gave sad summaries of the victims' lives and their families.

The Press on the same date was at a disadvantage, since the story was already reported. But it made up for that by interviewing anyone who witnessed the crime, or saw the truck on its route to the warehouse. It was there that I found my connection. Paul Stedman, whose store was next to the savings and loan, witnessed the murder-robbery. Like everyone else interviewed, he expressed horror but said little that was substantive.

Now I knew Roscoe's source for 65.

I turned to the May 10 issue. A plane crash in Chicago. According to the supplementary column, Penn was one of two local persons who died. His present employment and residence were listed, as was, ironically, his wife as sole survivor.

The details, if contemplated, were unpleasant, for the plane crashed on takeoff, bursting into flames. Three people, burned, managed to escape and were wandering on the field.

Could Penn have survived? I tossed the idea aside. The FAA would account for every body and its identification. Penn was dead.

All right. If Stedman was Roscoe's A, and Penn was B, who the hell was D?

I found a pay phone and called Al Burke in homicide. Told him I needed to know if anyone was ever charged for the armored-car murders ten years ago. He was curious but didn't push me and said he would need to call back. I asked him to call me at home that night.

It was time to see the Larches again.

At the low spot in the turn at the bottom of the hill in the woods below the house, Leslie Larch was standing beside a red MG-TC, a beautiful old angular creation that had just come to some slight misery. I braked gently, feeling the slide of mud and snow beneath me.

"Looks like I happened along at the right time," I said as I closed the car door.

From above a red, white and blue geometrically printed scarf she gave me a bright smile that indicated she was not only relieved but glad to see me.

"I'm afraid I tried to take that curve too fast." She raised her shoulders and eyebrows as one. "Now I can't get out."

I walked behind the car. Some paint was scraped from the left rear fender where it had brushed a tree, but it wasn't dented. Her problem, though, was a rock she'd hung the axle on.

Standing up, I brushed my hands and overcoat. "You need a tow truck or a shovel. Come on and get in; we can get one or the other up at the house."

"Can you get around me?" Her tone was injured, but her face remained bright.

"Yes." I nodded. "It's tight, but we can get through."

"Ben will be furious. It's my car, but his baby." Now her voice was earnest.

"It doesn't look as though it will require much, though no body work comes cheap now." I meant what I said, but passed it on casually, knowing she could afford to have her car repaired, rebuilt, or reassembled from parts.

"It's not the money, God knows. He'll simply remind me, as he does so well, how careless I am."

"Are you careless?" I meant to be light with her, but for the first time she was serious with me.

"No!"

She was standing in front of her car, away from me, as I walked back to the driver's side. I turned my head to her and smiled.

She laughed. "You didn't expect an answer."

I shrugged. "Come on."

When she got in she put her hands in her lap. "I'm sorry about the other night."

"What do you mean?"

"We weren't very hospitable when I came in."

"Smelling like a dog?"

"Yes, if you insist, too."

"No, I don't, and I wasn't bothered." I turned the engine over.

"Well, Ben was rather unpleasant. He doesn't really like the dogs."

"He gave me the opposite impression when he first told me what you did."

We squeezed by with a foot to spare between us and the nearest tree. I left it in low as we went up the hill.

"But not the other night." She couldn't let the subject drop.

"I'm not surprised. He wants me busy, with something to take care of that doesn't bother him. So he approves publicly. But he wishes it were something more refined than dogs."

"Perhaps this whole thing with the skeleton has upset him."

"Oh, it has, but that isn't what's bothering him about me." Her candor held no embarrassment for her.

"Has it really upset him?"

"Yes. And so have you."

"I'm sorry to hear that. Maybe he's generally nervous."

She paused, then went on. "No, not usually. He told me that you were necessary but unnerving."

"Well, I've been called worse. I could even accept that as a compliment. Is that all he said?"

"Except for worrying about his mother and occasionally wondering what you may be finding."

The hillside had a couple of bare spots on it but otherwise was crusted white, with blades of brown grass sticking through. We were almost to the top and the house.

"Does he worry about her?"

"Yes, but I don't mind, if that's what you want to know." She paused as though awaiting an answer, but when I said nothing she went on. "They've been close, always, but I like her. She's strong and, despite what Bob may have said of her feelings for his father, capable of real kindness. Ben may not like my dogs, but she approves of my independent business."

No need to speak of the specific feelings Mrs. Larch had expressed to me for her husband. Nor did I mention that she might have an ulterior motive for approving of the dogs. Then again, my speculation could be wrong.

"Are your husband and his mother at home?"

"Ben's out. He said he'd be home for lunch. Park by the front door."

"Just in time to see the tow truck in action."

"Yes, damn."

"Is Bob here?"

"Frankly, who knows?"

"Or cares?"

"That's not fair, under the present circumstances."

I wondered if she meant the skeleton or the car. "Your tone brought it out."

She nodded. "Okay. Let's leave it that I don't know where he is."

"Okay with me," I said.

"Come on in. I'll get Mrs. Larch and then make my call."

She opened the car door and hopped up the steps two at a time. She had very thin legs, almost too thin. I got out and followed her into the house through the door she'd left open. She came back from the library, leaving its door open. I closed the front door.

"She must be upstairs. I'll be right back." Again she took the stairs as if in a race.

I stood in the middle of the hall, literally twiddling my thumbs, when the maid came out.

"I came in with Mrs. Larch's daughter-in-law." Feeling slightly foolish, I pointed upstairs. She stared at me as if on the second half of a double take and walked out. A minute later Leslie came back.

"She's dressing and said for you to wait in the library. Oh, yes, Bob isn't here. I checked."

"You're very efficient."

"Know where he is?"

"No. But he's not in sight."

She smiled pleasantly, with her whole face, as she had when I pulled up on the drive. Then she took off her scarf and coat and put them in the closet.

"Give me yours. I've got to make that call yet." She enjoyed the effect of her efficiency. In still another jumper, blue herringbone, and white blouse with a bib, she might have been part of Mary's office.

I left her to her call and walked back to the library, paused inside the door to admire the vase Mrs. Larch had pointed out and turned on the light over it. It was perfect, exquisite, as she said, in shape and frieze. Like a human personality, its gorgeous exterior removed one's mind from the pottery beneath. Even if one got through its painted exterior, the shape was a separate quality, still obscure, for the glaze covered it all. Like peeling off layers of personality, the vase had layers to penetrate. And what if one peeled back all the layers? Could he be assured of reality, of fact, much less truth? Perhaps the truth was in the exterior; maybe one only destroyed. I turned off the light. But what if one didn't try to understand? That was the difference between the vase and a person. The vase would be destroyed because its essence was its totality, but the human was more durable and more difficult. So we keep peeling at the layers of ourselves and of others, in some des-

perate hope of essence. And often the peeling is resisted.
I had time to look over the books her first husband had collected before Mrs. Larch came down. But the steps I heard as I put back the first volume to a first-edition of *Tom Jones* were Leslie's.

"They were very nice. A man will be right over. I suppose everyone is simply curious to come in since the skeleton was found."

"Speaking of which, do you know anything about Ellen Penn?"

"Not really. She was before my time."

"Where she went to college?"

"To college?" She laughed and put her hands to her slim waist. "What do you need to know that for?"

"It might help me to find her."

"I think I'll go before you make sense and get me involved."

"Perhaps you're right. You may be happier not knowing. Do you need a ride down the hill?"

"No, thanks. I'm grateful you came along when you did. If I walk, and if a man is on the way out, we just might get there at the same time. You come back for a drink some evening; you owe me that after the other night."

"Very good projection."

She gave me the same open smile and left without saying more. I went back to perusing the collection. Now that Leslie seemed to accept me, she was so much more cheerful than anyone else in the house that she took on a sense of youth in a retirement village. Not only was the difference increasingly clear, but the contrast in mood made her seem younger. She may have created an illusion, but it served a real purpose finally. It may have been this cheerfulness to which Mrs. Larch alluded when she approved of Leslie the first night I was here.

I hadn't proceeded far down the shelves when Mrs. Larch came in, wearing a yellow knit dress, a hand-knit white cardigan over her shoulders.

"It's a fine collection, isn't it?"

"I'm not a bibliophile, but few who are could begin to afford this collection."

"It isn't just the cost. There are hundreds of people who could afford these. It was Mr. Larch's discernment. And his integrity. He wouldn't buy for the sake of owning. The books were to be used." She walked to my side and by facing the books forced me to turn beside her. "You see that shelf—to our right and one above your head? Those copies of *Don Quixote* he bought after he taught himself Spanish. He bought the leftmost copy before he learned to read Spanish, but left it in the wrapping paper until he could use it." She walked away from me toward the center of the room.

"The French and German works he had been collecting since college. I think his only real disappointment with his collection was that he never learned Russian."

"So he never read Dostoevski."

"In translations. But he kept those in the study or bedroom. They were not a part of the collection." She had been watching me and now smiled, a guileless, superior smile. "All this must seem snobbish to you."

"Faintly, but I have to admit that the feeling may come partly from envy. It is an admirable collection, and I would also admit that the reason for collecting as you described it was admirable. It's interesting that his taste reveals both aesthetic and pragmatic interests—unlike, say, that vase which I was also admiring before you came in."

"Come, let's sit down." She gestured toward the couches. She took a corner seat again, so I sat on the other couch, and we faced each other at angles.

"I should tell you that when I heard you were here I was not pleased. But now I have mixed feelings. You're a very observant young man. I think my husband would have liked you."

"I'm glad you don't think of me as an enemy."

"But you did come here for a reason. Something other than the examination of books."

"I might as well get to that. How well did you know Mr. Stedman when you married him?"

She tipped her head in a way that was coy, though I was sure that idea never entered her head.

"To make a comparison that is the antithesis of yours between the books and the vase, Paul would have owned the translations in the other room, and not read them." The last phrase was heavy with sarcasm.

"Then he was a materialist."

"Now please understand me. I hate Paul Stedman for what he did to me—I'll never forget it." She paused, more for emphasis than composure. "But I've always been taught to be reasonable, and I believe that. Reason says he was no more materialistic than I was or am. I enjoy comforts now and I expect to until I die. I thought he would be a pleasure—attractive, articulate, attentive. He knew I was a means to an end, and I felt the same about him."

She was admitting, as best she could, her own recalled lust. Stedman was younger and by her own words attractive. It was even more interesting that in her age and bitterness she could recall and admit her desire.

"Paul was ambitious and not without ability. So I only helped it along."

"Does that mean you wanted to share his business life?"

"No, oh no!" She shook her head vigorously. "I'm of an old school that says my place is here. But because I had the money, I was willing to finance ventures."

"Such as the boutiques?"

"Of course. I told you that before."

"Did it ever occur to you to distrust your husband?"

"You mean before he left? Yes, I think he could be ruthless if forced to."

I wondered if she was being fair now, or admiring.

"Were there any specific reasons?"

"Yes, the reason he left my family's company. He started to intrude on others' accounts."

"Sales accounts?"

She nodded. "Probably to make himself look good. He was in the family and knew how to suggest to some customers that this might be of use in any deals they made with him."

"What about in his business with Penn? Did he ever indicate his ambitions there?"

"Why do you ask?"

"Someone in the business may have been involved in armed robbery and murder."

"If Paul was, he was more daring and exciting than I realized. Can you tell me more, or are you only going to tell Bob, since he's your client?" There was condescension in the last phrase.

"I'll tell him, but there is no reason not to tell you, since you're being so helpful."

She nodded, her lips forming a superior smile.

"A month before your husband disappeared, there was an armed robbery in the bank next to his store."

"And you think he was involved." She crossed her legs.

"Perhaps. One lead I have suggests that is possible."

"But he wouldn't kill."

"Not even for one-fourth of $750,000?"

"He had my money."

I said nothing.

Then she realized, "But he was leaving me." She paused, looked at me, then out the window on the dripping trees. "You must know I don't make a very good witness. If you want to be convinced of Paul's guilt for those crimes, you must know I hate him enough to accuse him. So what you must be doing is looking for my reactions, not just my answers. Do I disappoint you?" There was contentment in turning the questions back to me.

"Would you like to know you surprise me?"

"By my detachment?"

"Yes. And by the reversal you have taken. The other day you were very bitter about Paul Stedman."

"I still am. But Ben and I had a talk, and he showed me that the way to settle this . . . problem . . . is to help."

"Have you talked freely to Lieutenant Carlson?"

"Ben has for me. I've depended a great deal on his advice. He's showing his father's wisdom. He's realized how hard this has been for me, and he's taken on much of the responsibility."

"But you are talking to me."

"Let's say it is something I owe Bob, or even that I see a difference between you and Lieutenant Carlson."

"Will Ben be back soon?"

"Yes; he went on some personal errands."

"Do you know anything about Ellen Penn?"

"Not much. What did you want to know?"

"I wondered if you knew where she went to college."

"I don't even know if she did go." The scorn was distinct. Perhaps Ben hadn't mentioned Ellen when he told his mother to cooperate. Then with self-conscious effort she restrained herself. "How is that going to help explain what happened?"

"It may not. But any lead from the past might help. Do you know about her family?"

"We saw each other about six times in our lives, and believe it or not, our indifference was mutual. Neither do I remember asking, nor do I remember any comments about her family." She drummed her fingers across the table once. "You asked those questions in a strange order. You're more interested in her college career."

I smiled. "You're a quick woman, Mrs. Larch. Again, my lead. All I'd prefer to tell you is that it's not a very good lead because it's old. Is Bob around? I'd like to tell him these same things."

"He wasn't home last night. He's not very useful right now, considering that he started it all."

Bringing up Ellen Penn had made her edgy.

"Started it?"

"By calling you and the police."

"It hasn't been easy for him, I imagine. Do you have any idea where he was last night?"

"No. He hasn't any close friends, not here or at college. But he has money and a car, so he could have gone anywhere. Do you wish to wait for Ben?"

"If you don't mind."

"Can we talk of other matters? My family is still something I would like to keep as private as possible."

I nodded and we sat for a moment in silence. I looked about the room. "Who built this house?"

"My grandfather. It's the last of three he built. We had one at Bar Harbor and one at Palm Beach. We've always lived together. My father was one of two sons—his brother died of influenza in childhood—and I was an only child. Ben is the first one to leave this house."

Not to go very far, I thought. "That sounds like an enviable, comfortable life."

"It was, it was. Both my husbands were ambitious, but in different ways. Ben—senior—was on his own once I helped out."

"In the family business?"

"Naturally."

"You must have been disappointed that Ben didn't follow his father."

"I was. After Paul, I would have preferred that we stick to our own affairs."

"But you supported him?"

She raised her eyebrows. "Financially? Of course. Certainly if I did so for Paul, I could for my son."

"And what of Bob?"

"He hasn't any purpose yet. Let him finish college." Her voice was slightly harsh, which she instantly realized and shifted in tone. "Then, I would do anything for him." I believed her. She'd told me before that she felt sorry for him, and I think she did, but she had a hard time separating him from his father.

"I've a board meeting to go to, Mr. Stuart, so if you don't have any further questions . . ."

"The company?"

"No, a hospital."

"Then I'll be going." I shifted my feet to stand.

"Don't you want to wait for Ben?"

"That won't be necessary. I won't disturb him. You've been very helpful." More than he might be, too, I'd reconsidered, after a quarrel with his wife.

"One more thing, Mr. Stuart. I think you've heard far too much about our family already, and as you can tell, what you know is not pleasant for me."

"If you want the police to handle the matter, you can tell Bob to fire me."

"Fire? Heavens, no! You work for him. Even if he isn't paying you—or is he?"

"Not yet. Except for a retainer."

"Well, I'll see that he pays you and advances you expenses. He needs to know."

"And do you?"

"Not really. I'm happy to know as little of this as possible. And that brings me back to my original point. Couldn't you follow some of these other leads? Ellen Penn and robbery, or what else. Give me a rest from my family's most unpleasant hour."

Always her family; never simply her. Most likely she projected; perhaps she had no identity beyond her family history.

"Certainly. I think my leads are there anyway. The skeleton has offered no clues. I will have to talk to Bob further. After all, he is my client."

"Yes." She seemed relieved that I had agreed. "Meanwhile, since you are here, could I advance some expense money?"

She saw the hesitation on my face.

"It's not a bribe. Where do you think Bob gets his money? If you prefer it come from his hands, suit yourself."

"No, I apologize for appearing to distrust you." She was right, too; for a moment I had suspected her of wanting to be rid of me entirely. "I'll tell Bob you advanced expenses."

"Five hundred dollars?"

"That's fine." The amount didn't matter so much as the relationship between the two of us.

She went to her desk, took out her checkbook and fountain pen, wrote out the check, then waved it to dry. I walked over to the desk and stood before her.

"What do you plan to do now?" she asked as she handed me the check.

"I'm not sure." I smiled. "For five hundred dollars you should receive some assurance, but I can't make a promise. I need to hunt for my next move."

"I hope you find it." Her voice was pleasant, mildly encouraging, self-assured now.

"Would you leave a message with the maid for Bob to call me at home?"

"Yes, of course."

Whether she was actually going out or not, though she had no reason to lie, I knew it was time for me to leave. She came to the door with me to say good-by.

At the foot of the hill, the tow truck hadn't arrived but Ben Larch had. He and Leslie were sitting in the front seat of his car. He was talking to her, but she was staring ahead. Neither looked at me as I passed.

When I got home I fixed a sandwich, opened a beer, and read Roscoe's notes again.

11

In his small hand, for 172, Roscoe had written the one lead he left me: "1-6, Exp. 3." The figures indicated that he had found her college, but he failed to note what it was. 1-6, Exp. 3 had to do with Ellen Penn's job, but they could refer to geography, or salary classification, or could even be Roscoe's own code. But I decided to go for the obvious. I assumed that Ellen taught school, had gone to a teachers college, and the note meant grades 1-6 with third-grade experience. But I could never phone every teachers college. I couldn't avoid calling Ben Larch, hoping he would be in a better mood after a night's sleep, to see if he knew. He answered in a voice that indicated his displeasure over the MG hadn't abated.

"What do you want, Stuart?"

"Help me find Ellen Penn."

There was a pause of several seconds. "What? How would I be able to do that? I've got too much on my mind."

"The MG?"

"Yes, that's right; you saw it. I know I may seem petty, but that's a damn fine car. Or at least it was."

"It looked to me as though a little paint would make it right again." I was irritated by his concern over the scratch on his car. He was petty.

"Well . . . oh, never mind. What did you want?"

"Do you know where she went to college?"

"Why the hell do you need to know that?"

"I think that's how Roscoe found her."

"What?"

"Through a placement office, I imagine."

Again he paused. "I see. Well, he never told me, or if he did, I forgot. Sorry, I can't help you. Now if there isn't anything else, I'm going to go back to getting some telephone estimates on putting this car back in shape."

I said no, cursed his stupidity and my bad luck under my breath, and hung up. Larch had been my best hope, since Roscoe just might have told him something he didn't tell Mrs. Larch. Now I had only Bolen and Roscoe's sister, who said he never told her anything. Instead of trying them I decided to do some finger work.

The girl I reached at the personnel office of the Cleveland Public Schools was pleasant but tired. I told her Ellen Penn had applied for a job as my secretary and had said to feel free to check her work record, which included a period of teaching in the Cleveland schools.

"We don't give out that information on the phone."

"I know, but I've found one other discrepancy in her record, and if she's lied again I thought I could save myself a trip to your office."

I could hear her sigh as she thought the matter over. "When did she say she worked here?"

"Thanks a lot. 1965 to '67."

"You'll have to hold on. What was her name?"

I spelled it out, then waited for nearly five minutes.

"I think she lied to you again."

"That's too bad. She made a good impression until I started on these references. That's the only reason I decided to call you after the first lie I discovered."

"That's too bad. Hope you aren't too sore. It's hard getting a job these days. Especially in teaching."

In her sympathy for Ellen she missed the irrelevance of her last comment, but now she sounded interested. "Sorry I couldn't help."

"But you did." I thanked her and hung up. She had been a

help, in a discouraging way. The biggest system was eliminated. Now I could check the suburbs. I started on the east side, since that was where they had lived. An hour and a half later I lucked out. The girl had taken some coaxing, since she was afraid to act without her boss's approval and he was out of town. But Ellen Penn had taught there for one year.

"This is a great help, to know she was telling the truth after all. Can I ask you one more favor?"

"What is it?" She was apprehensive, as though I had threatened her job.

"Do you have her education record there?"

"Of course. We have complete vital information. But I can't release it. Even Mr. Harrington wouldn't give you that."

"Could you check one more thing for me? As another way of verifying her interview with me?" I could sense how pushed she felt, but I had to go on, and hope.

"Well . . . what was it you wanted to know?"

"She seemed well educated—articulate, that is—and claimed she had a master's degree from Columbia."

"Why, all her form shows is a B.S. from Texas North Central College." Her surprise let out the necessary information without allowing her to know what she had done.

"Then she did lie, after all."

"Perhaps she earned the degree after she left here."

"Maybe you're right. I'd better call New York. Thank you again."

She was so relieved to have the questions end that she thanked me.

I got up from my desk and retrieved a twenty-year-old copy of *American Colleges and Universities* that I had used when looking for a college; then I called Texas instead of New York.

I got the placement office, repeated my lie about her employment record, and made the connection I needed. Ellen Penn had last had her dossier sent to Adams, Massachusetts.

"But there's something strange. Her maiden name was Burns. Then her record shows Penn, but we sent her file off under the name of Walters."

"Maybe she liked her first husband and his name better, but too late. That sometimes happens."

"Yeah, you never know how good you have it until it's too late." The voice drawled as it lapsed into cliche.

"You're so right. Thanks again. You were a big help." A phrase I was tired of using.

I called a travel agent and found that Mohawk and American both had flights to Albany that afternoon or evening. I had him check American, the probable AA on Roscoe's sheet, and made a reservation.

I felt a lot better than I had when Larch gave me the cold shoulder earlier. Everything would fall into place.

Between ten-thirty and eleven that night I landed in Albany. After renting a car, I picked up route two and drove across the river to Troy, where I found a room.

12

At seven-thirty I awoke to the brilliant white wall of curtains across my motel room. I had slept hard and awakened suddenly, but everything was clear before me, just as the light made the room. I showered and had breakfast in the motel coffee shop, at a pace that was neither rapid nor casual. I knew it might still take me some time to find Stedman, that I might even be wrong, but I felt close and could afford to be patient.

The storms that had covered us had gone on across upstate New York into New England, leaving a foot or more of snow there. But while the city was the same as it was at home, slushy and dirty, the countryside was a series of calendar scenes. Route two, cleared and heavily sanded, was easy going, and the drive over the Berkshires was as beautiful as ever. It would be crowded at the ski resorts this weekend, and with any luck they could look forward to a long season. I'd lived in New England for seven years of college and law school and recalled its seasonal tourist attractions. We had scorned the leaf lookers and snow bunnies, but now I could see why they needed to leave the city, if only for an afternoon. One had only to live in a city for a short time to know the need to get away. The only point we may have been right to scorn was the futility of most of the escapism, but even then we should have felt pity. But compassion is a rare quality at that age.

I drove through Williamstown and North Adams, then turned south. In Adams it took a while, but I learned that Ellen Walters had quit her job, according to the records, six years before. Not according to the record but to the fifty-year-old woman who searched the employment files for me, Ellen had quit only to help her husband with their hardware store in Exbridge, five miles away. She was helpful because I told her Ellen was sought regarding an inheritance. She didn't inquire, so I didn't have to explain how unpleasant the inheritance was. She gave me directions which involved little more than driving south for five miles to a town that took up both sides of the road for several yards. She added to say hello to Ellen and that Susan was glad to hear of her luck.

Exbridge had ten stores and a post office, the newest building. The hardware store announced itself with a plain sign that said hardware. It was in the center of the row of stores on the east side of the road, and the largest store. I parked across from it, heading south, and went in. A bell over the door tinkled. A man behind the counter down the left side of the store was helping a customer.

"I'll be right with you, mister."

It was Stedman, in his early fifties, but easily recognizable from Bob's photograph. He had made no attempt to disguise his appearance.

I said not to hurry and looked about. Ellen wasn't there. I walked back and forth over creaky wooden floors—past paints, chains, axe handles, fences, kitchen items, hunting and fishing equipment. What I listened to of their conversation was as much friendly and social as it was business, as they talked over chains and this Saturday night. Finally the man left and Stedman came over to me.

"Now, what can I help you with, mister?" The flat midwestern tone was still in his voice.

"A great deal, Mr. Stedman."

He visibly paled, as though in shock.

"My name is Stuart, and I was hired to find you."

Still he said nothing, and seemed to have regained none of the composure that was his only seconds before.

"Your son Bob hired me."

"I'm afraid you've. . . . "

"Made a mistake. No. I've seen your picture. The one of you and Bob fishing. He has secretly kept it for ten years."

Stedman was about my height, but with each passing second he seemed more stooped, as though the past were a literal weight upon him. But except for the graying of his cropped brown hair that he still brushed to the side and slightly over his forehead, and a few additional wrinkles about the eyes, he was unchanged until we spoke.

Finally, leaning back with both hands on the counter, he spoke. "Is Bob all right?"

"Yes."

When he said, "I realize that must seem feeble after ten years," I was glad I'd said nothing.

"You can't be completely surprised to see me."

"What do you mean?"

"The story of the headless skeleton was on the wire services."

"What . . . what about it?" He seemed genuinely puzzled, like a fighter who has gone one round too many. He shook his head, attempting to clear it. "In Cleveland? Yes . . . yes. It was in the *Eagle*."

"Did the story give any details?"

"No." He shook his head again. "No."

"It was found on your wife's property."

"Marian's?" He turned around to lean on the counter. "What's that got to do with me? It's all coming too fast. I don't understand."

"Because there was no head, there was no way to identify the body. Bob received a letter with instructions to dig there. He wanted me to find out if the body was yours, or if you'd put it there."

He turned his head toward me without moving his hands or shoulders. "And since I am alive, I must have put the body there."

"Possibly. But not necessarily."

"Thank you." There was no sarcasm in his voice. He was too

drained. He wiped the right sleeve of his red flannel shirt across his forehead.

"Where is Ellen Penn?"

"Ellie's at home. She'll have lunch for me soon." The despair hung from his words, as though this might be a final meal in this home.

He walked away, then walked back, pulling himself up to my height. "Can I ask a favor?"

"Try me."

"Can we meet you here tonight? Ellie and I will both be here."

"What's wrong with now?"

"Can't I spare her the shock you gave me? Let me tell her; let us talk." He was pleading. "Don't make me break up my store hours. All right, I'm begging. I want to hold on to what I have."

"What time?"

"I close at six. Six-thirty . . . there shouldn't be many people in town. You could come in the back." Now the words rushed out, just as though a new burst of hope had fired him, or perhaps possessed him.

"What assurance do I have that you won't run?"

"What I just told you. I don't want to lose what I have. We're settled here."

"I'll take a chance on you, but only because I can go to the police, who will put out an all-points bulletin on you for murder. If you run, I'll do that. Now, where do you live?"

"About a mile north of town. On the main highway. Anyone can tell you."

"You must realize you have a lot to explain."

"I know." He nodded over the cash register. "I'll tell you anything, only I've got to have a chance to think it over. To figure out where I am."

"Don't figure too much. I want straight answers. Something your son would also appreciate."

"I won't lie. And I'll bring Ellie." He turned away. "I don't know how to thank you, Mr. . . . " He came around the counter.

117

"Stuart."
"Stuart."
"Do you have any boots?"
"Boots?"
"For sale. I forgot to bring anything to protect my shoes from the snow."
"Oh. Just some old-fashioned galoshes."
"That's fine. I wear an 11½ shoe."
"You'll need a large." He went about halfway down the left-side counter, climbed a ladder and reached a box off the top shelf.
"I'll just put them on. How much?"
He stared at me before saying, "Nine dollars," as though he couldn't believe me. Perhaps he couldn't believe anyone would buy anything now.
"Is there any place in town where I can get a room?"
"Mrs. Trumble's. About a quarter of a mile south of here."
I left him standing there in the middle of the floor and crossed the street to a diner–cigar store. A few minutes later, while I was waiting for some pork chops to brown, Stedman left in a late-model blue Ford pickup.

After I ate I bought a *Harper's* and a *New Yorker* at the counter and set out to find Mrs. Trumble, who was forty-five or so. I took a room, read a couple of articles, then dozed for a while. When I awoke I read the *New Yorker* profile on a painter who was unknown to me. As I watched the clock, I kept reading, and worried if I should have trusted Stedman. At five-fifteen I walked back to town to the diner. The bright sun had already set and in the cold dusk I wished I had driven. An owl hooted solemnly, regularly. It all seemed a pleasant change, a different world from the one I had left twenty-four hours before. I was glad to reach the diner, but the out-of-doors—cold, quiet—made me sympathetic to Stedman. I remembered I had sought something like this, only temporarily, several hundred miles south the previous week.

The diner closed at six, but the man behind the counter let me linger a few minutes over a second cup of coffee as he cleaned up, emptying the coffee urn and scraping his grill. He worked steadily, methodically and silently—anxious to go home. There had been no traffic on the highway for twenty minutes, so he had every reason to want to go home. As soon as he finished the grill I put down my cup and paid.

Outside, the air was clear and cold. A twin-engine plane, its running lights glowing, ground out an intrusive hum to the land below before droning into the distance and finally becoming inaudible. I crossed the highway, and suddenly my shadow disappeared as the lights in the diner went out. Up and down the rows of stores only a couple of lights glowed in the windows.

Behind the hardware store there was no pickup truck, but a light came from under a loading door. I pushed up the door and went in. Stedman was going over some account books in a small room immediately inside the storage area, but he looked up at the noises I made.

"I figured you could let yourself in. I haven't been getting very far with these, not since I expected you."

"Where is Ellen Penn?"

"I think you should call her by her right name—Walters."

"You're married?"

"I waited until I was sure Marian had divorced me."

"Where is your wife?"

"She'll be along. I gave her the truck after lunch. When I told her about you at lunch, she was too upset to come in this afternoon. She dropped me off." He stood up. "Let me hang up your coat."

I gave it to him, and he hung it on a coat tree in the corner, next to his mackinaw, while I took off the galoshes. I dropped them outside the door in the storage room, even though it wouldn't have hurt the floor to leave them anywhere.

"That's a nice coat. I haven't needed to dress like that in years."

I ignored that.

"Do you want to wait to answer my questions?"

"I can answer for both of us." He wiggled a pencil back and forth between his thumb and index finger. To do his work he had used only an old, low, green-glass-shaded desk light that illuminated a small area on the top of the desk. His face was slowly becoming visible in the dark green haze above the desk top.

"Where do you want me to start?" he asked.

"Anywhere. You must have given it some thought in the last few hours." I pulled up a curved-back wooden armchair that sat by the door, the kind I remember from college libraries.

"Well, I'll tell you about me, before I met Ellie. I had an obscure enough background and enough ambition to see a good chance in Marian and Inter-Lake Ore."

"You married her for her money?"

"Partly. She was also an attractive woman, and I was vain enough to believe I could fill a need in her life. I did, too, but only at heavy cost . . . to both of us. I learned over the ten years of our life together that I wasn't so good as my ambitions had led me to believe. I did an average job, made adequate sales, but was never ready to move to the top. That's not self-pity, just a fact. Ten years ago I might not have made that admission; now I'm happy enough that I don't mind."

"How did she feel about this inability?"

"Tolerant at first, because she loved me. Then unhappy, and finally angry that I wasn't a Ben Larch. We can't all be business and government leaders." Enough defensiveness remained to make his voice sarcastic.

I said, "No." Not so much because of the obvious truth in what he said, but because of his desire for a response. I wondered if he would ever be happy.

"We were happy for a while. Did she tell you that?" He was irritable; his voice quavered from feeling to feeling, as though he expected me to say no.

"Yes, she did."

"Well, I have to give her some credit."

"Time helps." I didn't yet want to say how she now felt.

"Perhaps we both came out for the best when I left."

"Perhaps."

"She was good about the business with Bill Penn." There was a trace of sentimental nostalgia in his voice. "The idea was good. I see now they even advertise in the *New Yorker*. The Purple Tree does, I mean. Who bought it—do you know?"

"Alec Bolen—for his daughter."

"He's like Ben Larch. Well, I'm not bitter now. They make it big—I've learned that about the world. And it's taken me the last twenty years to grasp the lesson." There was a slight, mocking laugh in his last sentence. His words said one thing and his voice another. Occasionally they met.

"But you were bitter once."

"At my failure." He sucked in air through clenched teeth, reliving the feeling so vividly and with such instant change from only a moment before that I wondered what was real for him. Was it just his business failure, or some other failure—his marriage perhaps, or the loss of a fortune?

"What about your son?"

"He's the one who suffered most. Isn't he?"

"Yes. He's never had the attention any human needs."

"Not even from Marian?"

"No. She told me she felt guilty, but she'd never been able to feel for him what he deserved."

"Then she does blame me. You said she didn't."

"No. I said she told me your marriage had been good for a while."

"So Bob suffers." He leaned back in his chair and raised his left hand to his forehead. Outside, a car ground over the snow and ice; then a motor stopped. The intrusion roused him from his momentary drift into himself. "I'll be right back." In the storage room outside his office a light went on; then he raised the overhead door.

"He's here," I heard him say.

I looked at my watch. It was quarter to seven. They came to the office door. He was holding her shoulders.

"Ellie, this is Mr. Stuart. I told you. We were talking about Bob just now."

She was about forty, still very attractive, even in brown corduroy pants and a waterproof parka. Her age was in the lines in her thin face, for her hair was still light brown, but the lines were drawn tight now. She seemed to have suffered more than her husband, or she showed her feelings even more clearly than he did.

He guided her by both shoulders into the room and over to his chair. The tension in her body was visible, and I thought he must have felt the tightened muscles of her upper arm as he moved her. He went back to the storeroom for a straight-backed chair for himself. She kept her coat on.

"Should I heat some water for coffee?" he asked her, but she only shook her head.

She cleared her throat and we both waited for her to speak. Finally, after clearing it a second time, she looked to me. "Are you here to blackmail us?"

"No."

"I told you he's here because of Bob."

"And I think he must know a great deal just to be here." Her voice had a shrill edge on it.

"I do. But what I know is confidential."

"Who else knows about us?"

"Where you are? No one." I wanted to reassure her.

"And who else knows you're looking for us?"

"The Larches."

"Can't they leave us alone?"

"They would. It's the skeleton I told your husband about that brought your new life up."

"What skeleton?"

I looked at Stedman. "A skeleton was found on the Larch estate a few days ago."

"What does that have to do with us?"

"Everything," I said.

"No, it doesn't, Mr. Stuart," said Stedman. "Because I didn't send that letter to Bob."

That possibility had always existed, but it had seemed remote since this afternoon, when he had not denied it, only the murder.

"Why didn't you say so this afternoon?"

"I must have believed you were more concerned over whether I was a murderer. I don't know for sure."

"I can't be sure."

"He's no murderer." She hovered between anger and tears.

"We'll make him see that, Ellie."

"How?" I asked.

"Do you have the letters I sent? How was I supposed to have sent them?"

"You know that the more I tell you, the more difficult it will be to prove your version."

"I can't help that." He paused. "If I don't know what I've done, I can't defend myself."

I decided to try him. "Here's a copy of the letter to your son."

He took it, read it under the green light, and gave it to his wife.

"It's not signed."

"But that could be a cover for you as much as for anyone else."

"I see." There was some anger in his voice because I was unconvinced. "Let me read it again."

His wife gave it to him, then looked at me. "Don't you think a father would say something more personal to his son?"

"That occurred to me at first, too. But then I realized he would also be cutting all his connections and might not want to be personal. The distance could have been planned for that reason."

"Don't you believe anything we say?" she cried.

"Give me something substantial."

"All right, granting all you say! Whom would I have killed and buried? And why there? I've had no desire to go back. I haven't gone back," he added to correct himself.

"Do you know a man named Dwight Roscoe?"

They looked at each other, wondering what to say. Stedman dropped the letter on the desk.

"No," said Ellen. Her left hand grasped the arm of her chair rigidly.

"That's not true, dear. And he can see that. Can't you, Mr. Stuart?" His voice was calm, almost hushed.

I nodded.

"I remember him. I should say I can't forget him. He's about my age. We saw him almost ten years ago. After we moved here, but before we bought the store. He was a detective, like you, hired to find us."

"What did he tell you?"

"That Marian hired him." She was angry, more than she had been before.

"Take it easy. That's ten years ago," he told her.

"She wouldn't leave us alone. Don't you see that, Paul? She still won't."

"I'm not working for her but for Bob. And no one would ever have bothered you again if it weren't for the letter your husband claims he didn't send."

"I didn't."

"All right. But let's not go back to that for now."

"Roscoe found you, and although he had been making regular reports to Mrs. Larch, she says he never told her where you were."

"She's probably telling the truth, then." He looked relieved.

"Why?"

"Because we asked him not to. Just the way I'm begging you not to." Ellen was straining to keep control, feeling none of the relief Stedman showed. "I told him we weren't going back. That no one could force us to. Bill was dead by then, and Paul and I had decided to weather whatever pressure might be used on us. We didn't want their money." Her voice was getting higher. "We wanted to be left in peace."

"Why do you think we changed our name? We were afraid of someone like Roscoe or you."

"You were afraid, but you tell me he just walked away and never reported finding you?"

"Yes." His voice was as flat as if he were giving the temperature.

"Don't you see?" she added. "We can't pay anything now, so how could we pay him ten years ago? We had even less then."

"How did you buy the store?"

"We saved. And it's mortgaged."

"What about armed robbery and murder?"

With that he suddenly broke, like someone stripped of his last saving illusion. His heavy breathing made Ellen turn to him and prevented her speaking.

"You've checked a lot."

"Roscoe did most of the leg work. I used his file on you and did a little more."

"What do you need to know?"

"You were a witness, but in Roscoe's file there was someone else who was mixed up in both. I wondered why another person who seemed to be involved in the robbery was mentioned in his file on you two." Without telling him I knew that Roscoe hadn't mentioned him as a suspect, I took an opposite approach. "I decided you might have been in on the robbery and murders." He tried to speak, but I went on, "Not the action, but the planning."

"Wha . . ."

"That could have given you enough to pay him off. And buy the store."

"What do I need to do? Show you a mortgage? Did you ever find Roscoe? What is this file?"

"You could have killed him, too. He's been missing since he saw you."

"I'm going to tell you what I told him. Maybe that got him killed, but I didn't kill him." He took a breath. "I saw that robbery, and I recognized one of the robbers even in his disguise. His hat and glasses."

"Penn?"

"Bill? No. A clerk who had worked for us named Frank Ashe."

"And you didn't go to the police?"

"No. I was wrong in what I did."

"You're damned right. Three men were murdered."

"Don't you talk to him like that. He did it for us."

"I was there, Stuart. I saw those men die. I can still see them."

"But why didn't you tell the police?"

"For us, just as she said. We'd already made our plans to run away. It was dumb luck that made me see the robbery; it was even Bill's afternoon to be there."

"I'm responsible. Paul agonized for days before I convinced him it would be better not to go in."

"It's not her fault. I decided for myself."

"I talked you into it, Paul."

He simply shook his head.

"So you let the murders of three men go unsolved. You certainly were among the first of the uninvolved."

"I had to choose for us," he shouted. He got out of his chair and paced. "I thought the murders would be solved. There was a large reward and an angry city."

"So there was no need to put off your flight to domestic bliss."

"We had it coming. You don't know what Bill and Marian were like." She stood up and went to him.

"I've met Mrs. Larch. She's strong but not unbeatable."

"You're not married to her," he said lamely. "You don't know what her kind of power is, or her family's power."

"Did you tell Roscoe this?"

"No. He already knew about Ashe—I mean that he worked for us—because he'd been looking into our pasts to find us."

"Did he tell you Ashe might have been in on the robbery?"

"That he had a criminal record and might have taken the job with us to help plan the robbery."

"And you said nothing, even though the killers hadn't been caught."

He only nodded.

"You're one hell of a person. You walked out as a witness of three murders because of a possible inconvenience, and left a son—I suppose, to cut down the chance you would be found."

Neither said anything. Then she spoke, shaking her head as she did, "You'll never know what we went through, never."

I didn't feel like answering her.

"What are you going to say?" Paul asked finally.

"I think it's time to come out of hiding."

"Our lives were hell. What good will it do to dig up the past?" She was angry and imploring at the same time. "Bill and I had no marriage, long before I met Paul, and now Bill is dead. And Marian would dominate Paul's life till his dying day. She wanted regular reports on how he spent his time at the business." She sliced downward through the air with her opened right hand. "Why, he couldn't even go to work without her calling him or dropping by. The whole thing was intolerable until we found each other."

"Very romantic. So you decided to do just what you had disapproved—use people, even to the point of murder. Have you ever compared your values with those of the people you condemn?"

I got up and walked back and forth. I went over to the single window in the office, on the back wall, and leaned with my right hand on the dusty sill. They were both looking at the floor. A tractor-trailer roared through town, vibrating the floor beneath us. The pool of green light on the desk wavered.

"Well, what's it to be?" I said. "Me or the police? It would be better to make voluntary statements. I have enough money to buy our plane tickets from Albany to Cleveland."

"We'd . . . " He'd stopped, almost as though he had nothing to say.

"You've got a son who'd like to see you. He may not love you, but he wants to know if you're alive. Right now he's alone and screwed up. No one has seen him for three days. Frankly, I'd rather be looking for him."

"You're not being fair to Paul."

"Fair? Now is hardly the time to talk about fair. And you two are hardly the ones—you're as self-centered as you say any of the Larches are."

I was thoroughly sick of the whole affair. They were just middle-class versions of Mrs. Larch—life is pleasant, secure, don't change it. Instead of an estate they had a hardware store, and a life, as Stedman had said earlier today, they didn't want to leave. Only Bob and Leslie, the outcasts, the second string, seemed worthwhile to me. I decided that when I got them back I'd go to the Cleveland police with them and get out. The police could sort out the criminal charges; the family could sort out itself.

"Well?" I said.

"You're right." He nodded his head. "I should see Bob. None of this will be easy, but if you can find us, others will. Will you go back with us?"

I sighed. "That's why I'm here."

"Could we go into the other room for a minute, Mr. Stuart?"

"I'll go, Paul."

"No, we're both up. You sit still, dear."

He led the way into the storeroom without an answer from me. Inside the storeroom door he turned on a light and looked back at me. I pulled myself away from the sill. Maybe he wanted to leave her behind and make the trip alone with me.

Then it happened.

Inside the store there were counters on both sides of the door we had come through. The lights were out. He started to turn to his right, as though to turn them on. Then he turned back on me, pivoting to his left. I could see the white line extending from his hand into the darkness of the room. The thoughts flashed like tiny explosions across my brain.

Axe handle . . .

   Duck . . .

      Lunge . . .

I made the mistake of putting up my left arm and dodging the blow by moving back. But I had trapped myself against the door jamb. I tried to block the blow at my head, and managed to let my forearm take the blow full force. Everything was shattered into fractions of a second; I thought I could hear a stopwatch ticking its particles of time. In one movement of the sweephand my arm cracked; another and the pain shot down my arm to my shoulder and into my neck. Then I realized he had managed to strike the left rear side of my head in the glance of the axe handle off my arm. Simultaneously my left arm fell to my side and I began to crumple.

He must have known the blow was glancing, because in two more ticks of the watch, as I heard "Paul!" shouted, he raised the handle again and brought it down on my already collapsing body.

13

When I came to I was propped against a tree, my right shoulder braced against a split in the trunk. But it was several minutes before I knew that.

All I could be certain of at first was the pain in my left arm. The forearm was one sharp, continuous hurt that flowed into a throb in the upper arm, where I felt someone was applying a low voltage alternating current. Several minutes passed before I forced myself to realize there was more to me than my left arm. Gradually I defined the pain for myself and realized that my head, too, was pounding, on the left side. I started to raise my hand to feel the side of my head but stopped as the pain rebelled against my effort.

Only then did I realize I was sitting, but not where. I tried to look around me, but everything was dark. The effort to move my right arm was less painful, and no less difficult. The damned thing wouldn't move. The sudden sense of helplessness was less bearable than the pain. I could tell myself that pain would stop, but helplessness would not. Then, somehow, the two points connected for me: I was helpless because of the pain. The darkness I groped with inside was darker than that around me. The frustration built, but no more connections. I think I passed out again.

When I came around again, the night seemed clearer, though the real difference was probably in me. All around me I could make out only dark shapes—the rough, tangled shapes of branches, vines and bracken. There was no light anywhere, except in the stars—absolutely cold and distant—and in the half-moon that hung between still gray clouds. Actually I was more alive to the pain, because I was conscious now, not shrouded in semiconscious frustration. But because I could see again, and was not trapped, senseless, in a helpless self, I could stand the pain.

It was then that I realized where I was—in a general way. I moved my right hand away from the tree. No pain there. Okay. Time to try the damage to the other arm. The movement shocked me back into reality. No use in the left arm, so I felt my head with my right hand. The fingers all moved independently, but I could feel nothing other than the sore place along the left side of my head. What the hell, I was wearing gloves. My gloves. I stared, incredulous.

Walters . . . Stedman had smashed my arm and head, I told myself, and dumped me in a woods. That was memory and present reality. But gloves? Then I saw the galoshes and finally realized the obvious—my coat. All my outer clothes were on me. First he'd tried to kill me and dispose of me, then he'd sheltered me. No, not me, himself, I decided. What better way to get rid of my clothes, any evidence of my presence, than to put them back on me? I looked around again and knew I was right. Almost behind me to my left was a low hill. In the spring, or whenever I was found, I would be an accident. I had left Mrs. Trumble's walking and was a victim of my own curiosity. Stumbling into the woods on a ramble, I had fallen. That meant I couldn't be too far from Exbridge. But I had no way of being certain that Stedman thought the same way. I forced myself up, reminding myself that if I didn't get out of here, it wouldn't matter what Stedman thought.

The trees made a net over my head as I bent my head back and pressed my shoulders, neck and head against the bark of the trunk and pushed myself up with my feet. I felt I was doing some silly game at a party. Only I was the prize, for I had to save myself. Then I was standing, and the net hadn't entrapped me. But which way to go? I couldn't get back down to crawl around in semidarkness looking for their footprints in the snow. I looked over the dark shapes of land and trees for a clue. I decided they had brought me in through a flat space that narrowed to a gully. It would have been too hard to carry me down the hill of my accident. I peered down that way for tracks in the white snow; they were where I had thought, so I walked toward the gully. I brushed a tree with my left arm and groaned aloud. Be more careful, or you may not get out.

As I walked I came back to life; except for my broken arm and bruised skull I felt alive. My new consciousness was unfortunate, for I grew cold, even in my coat, boots, and gloves. Had they meant to protect me from the cold? Doubtful. I was safer dead. Better stop speculating and get out of the woods. When I came out of the gully I was relieved, for there was a field, plowed under, just a few dozen yards ahead through the trees. I stayed with the tracks as I could see them and was grateful that it wasn't snowing. Once I was in the field, the tracks made a clear slice across the open surface and were easy to follow in the unshaded expanse. I was glad to see I had been hard to carry, though I took small comfort in the fact that he had dropped me each time he stumbled. The footprints ended at a one lane road that cut through the field.

I felt dizzy from walking and was tempted to sit down on the mound beside a drainage ditch. But the memories of standing up, of the effort by my right side and the pain down my left stopped me. I followed the tire tracks, and soon it was clear that I had been wrong—I wasn't near Exbridge. The only pleasure I found in walking was knowing that the road had to end somewhere, and when it did, I could go to bed and forget—at least for a few hours or days. If only that skeleton had once taken a similar blow to the arm, I might not be here. It was a grim pleasure to think how I might have been identified simply by the wallet I could still feel in my hip pocket. I wouldn't inconvenience anyone.

Finally there was a highway. I had given up trying to judge distances a slow twenty minutes before. I had no idea where I was, but decided to head north, the way I had originally come. I could judge by my watch and the moon, and so followed my choice. Only no cars came by from either direction. The minutes dragged on. I knew I wasn't on a main road because it wasn't very wide, but it had been plowed and was sanded.

My left hand and arm were numb with cold, a blessing and a fear. I tried to move them slightly to restore feeling and control. The pain raced up my arm and into my neck and head. I wasn't about to freeze yet. I made myself think of Stedman, and my anger kept me going. Pain and anger are fine stimulants; only, like all stimulants, their effect is temporary. I wondered if they would hold out until a car came by. I was thinking of how I would like to use that axe handle on Stedman's solar plexus when a car came up behind me. It was going fast and was hardly steady on the road.

Bearing down on me at about seventy, it made me feel paranoid. I was trying to decide whether I could stand to dive into the snowbank or take my chance that it would go around me. Unfortunately, when the driver saw me he hit the brakes, and his car fishtailed down the road at me. I kept thinking, "Take your foot off the brake, you bastard." But he didn't. I waited until he was about thirty or forty yards away, when he seemed to have skidded into the left lane, then ran and dove at the snowbank on our right.

I remember how during a big snowstorm when I was a child the city plows would go through. At intersections, in order to clear large sections of road, they piled the snow high on one corner. They still do, but twenty-five years earlier the mounds of snow I dove over and into, slid down and tunneled through, seemed soft. I sank down a few inches on my right hip and shoulder before I came to a stunning halt that sent my left arm flapping. I think I screamed, but the noise may have been the sound of the brakes and tires skidding past me. I raised my head enough to see he'd come to a halt, with his left front bumper hooked into the snowbank.

I thought I was going to be sick and dropped my head on the snow. I was having the same problem I'd had before, trying to understand what my relationship was to the tree, to the outside world. All I could be certain of was myself—the nausea and pain. Then without lifting my head I heard a sick, metallic coughing and grinding of a motor that wouldn't turn over. It stopped, then after only a second started again. Was he going to leave me here? The abstract possibility of someone being left to die was always easy to grasp. Hadn't we grown up in a civilization of uninvolved people like Stedman? But to face the reality that one is about to be deserted to die is beyond belief. Suddenly my mouth dried. The saliva that flowed so freely as I felt nausea stopped. I had walked long enough alone to know I might not get out of this night safely alone. I might not get out—period. This first chance in all the minutes or hours I had been out had nearly finished me and was leaving, or trying to, at least.

The motor cranked again.

Then a door opened, and there was a hollow metallic sound. I wasn't sensate enough to identify the sound. Then it came again, this time in a series. A can; a can clattering over the road, muffled occasionally by sand and snow. Then the door slammed. "He's thrown out some cans," I thought. "What a hell of a time to be a litterbug." The battery ground again but failed to turn over the engine. "You've dumped your trash; now get out of here." I laughed to myself, almost without control. "Now they go out from the cities at night to get rid of their garbage."

Then I heard the footsteps, not distant, but practically beside me.

"Mister? You okay?" The voice was tentative, frightened, young.

"Yes," I mumbled.

"We didn't hit you, did we?"

"No." I started to shake my head, but pain prevented me. "I've got a broken arm."

"Let me get a flashlight." He ran back to the car, calling, "Tom."

I started to get up but thought better of it and decided to wait for their help. I was relieved.

Both of them came back. With the flashlight shining in my face, I blinked several times.

One of them whistled. "What happened to you, mister?"

"I was mugged."

"Out here?" His question was also an exclamation, and I didn't need to answer him.

"Which arm is broken?"

"The left." I managed a smile, since it hung limply at my side.

"Here, we'll try to get you up. Do you think you could walk to the car?"

"Yeah, I can make it."

They both stepped into the snow and took my weight so I could get up more easily than I had before. Their breath was stale beer under fresh cinnamon gum. I knew what kind of can I had heard.

Once we were out on the road I walked by myself toward their car, a blue Corvette.

"Can you give me a ride?"

"I'll ride in back, Tom."

"Okay. Get in, mister."

It wasn't easy getting down so low to a seat, but once I was in, I was comfortable by holding my left arm to my side.

"We've got to push it back onto the road."

I sat still, only occasionally watching them. Tom opened his door and guided the steering wheel with his right hand, bracing his body against the door frame and pushing his foot into the snow at the same time. The other boy stood in the snow in front of us and pushed. They rocked the car three times, then pushed it out. We were on the wrong side of the road.

The second boy crawled into the space behind the seat, and Tom got in. While the car was open I had smelled the gasoline—he'd flooded the engine—but now in the closed space I might have thought I was in a brewery. I could feel a six-pack at my feet.

"Where were you going?" asked Tom.

"Anywhere that has a doctor or a hospital. Where are you headed?"

"Williamstown."

"How far are we?"

"About twenty-five or thirty miles."

"Where's the nearest hospital?"

"Probably at North Adams."

"Try it again. It may not be flooded now."

He turned it over without pressing on the accelerator. The motor caught. He raced it twice. The car vibrated under its power.

"We'll take you to North Adams." He raced it again, but when he dropped into first he moved out slowly. By the time we were in high, the trees were flashing in and out of the headlights in rapid succession. I glanced over once, saw that he was doing between sixty-five and seventy and closed my eyes and leaned back. I dozed off for a few minutes as we raced through the night. Before I did, I realized we had passed no other cars and was glad they had come along, as hard on me as their arrival had been.

"Mister, mister!" The voice behind me was soft and urgent. "Are you okay?"

"Yes," I mumbled. "I fell asleep."

"I was afraid you . . . your breathing was . . . I couldn't hear it."

"Probably because of this engine." I smiled. Tom looked over at me, and I had the feeling in the darkness that he had taken my observation for praise and was pleased.

"Were you really mugged?"

"Let him rest, Neil."

"I just find that hard to believe."

I would too, in his place. But I'd decided to go along with the story I figured the Stedmans would put out if they needed to. By walking into town, as Mrs. Trumble and the cook in the diner could verify, I had made a kidnapping-mugging story possible. My wallet was still there, but I had no idea if the money was—probably not.

"Leave him alone; can't you see he needs to rest?"

"Yeah, sure."

So Neil asked no more questions, and I missed a chance to try out some answers. But I figured the story would work, if Stedman had taken my money.

They stopped at a gas station outside North Adams and got

directions to the hospital. The attendant looked at me through Tom's open window, the blue-white lights through the windshield illuminating my face. He whistled, and I realized why they had asked me if I was all right. The left side of my face must have been the mess it felt.

When they were a block from the hospital, Tom asked me if I wanted them to go in. He didn't sound anxious to stop.

When I said "No" there was relief in his voice.

"Are you sure? Where can we drop you?"

I decided there was no reason for them to be further involved. They had done their part. "Pull up near Emergency. I'll go from there."

He did. Both boys got out and came around to my side. I was warm now, and the pain seemed worse, but dull. The cold air was a shock. I decided to let it keep me awake, so I stood on the sidewalk and watched them drive out of sight, rather than let them watch me go inside. I'd told them to beat it for their own sakes first. The Corvette eased out of sight, and I walked through the emergency entrance.

The nurse at the desk was young, not particularly pretty, and appeared tired. She took one look at me and all traces of sleepiness disappeared.

The face I had yet to see tonight was having its effect on people. She got a resident, who took me back to an examining room. He'd noticed the arm hanging at my side and helped me with my gloves and coat. He started to roll up my shirtsleeve, then stopped.

"You might be more comfortable if I cut that sleeve."

"Go ahead. That's the least damage I've suffered tonight."

He smiled, picked up some surgical scissors and slit my sleeve.

There was a terrible bruise, spreading from my elbow almost to my wrist, but no bone protruding or pushing at the skin.

"It appears to be a simple fracture, but we'll have it X-rayed. Let me take a look at your head." He examined the left side of my head without touching it. "That should be X-rayed, too. Do you know what hit you?"

"An axe handle."

His eyes opened wider, then returned to their normal size. "Judging by where the one line ends, I'd say you were lucky not to have a broken jaw. You may have a skull fracture. And you may need a couple of stitches."

"I wouldn't be surprised." I stood up, felt dizzy and said so.

"Sit down in this." He turned to get a wheelchair from a corner and I blacked out. I didn't even hear myself hit the floor.

It was daylight, and I was sharing a hospital room with two other men. A fourth bed was empty. They were on the opposite wall, both eating breakfast.

The older of the two, a man in his fifties, turned his head when he heard me move. He suspended a spoonful of cereal over his tray. He sat on the edge of the bed in a hospital gown, one of those institutional uniforms that not only takes away all dignity, but identity too.

"How're you feeling?"

I mumbled, "Fine."

He nodded and lifted the cereal to his mouth. The other patient was a kid about eighteen who hadn't touched his food. He seemed to sulk in self-pity more than pain. He wore his own pajamas.

"They brought you in about three-thirty or four. What happened?" He had pushed his cereal aside and was peeling back the cover to a packet of jelly.

I started to answer him when I realized my left arm was in a cast, from my hand to my elbow. I lifted it. The pain was now only discomfort. Then I thought of my head and was aware of the pulling sensation on the left temple and cheek. I raised the skin of my cheek by wrinkling it and felt the bandage. Then I moved my jaw. It was okay. The mumble was from the thickness in the back of my throat. I coughed to clear it.

"Is there any water?"

"Not for you yet. Can you reach the buzzer? Never mind, I'll get it."

When a nurse finally answered the red light, he told her I wanted water. She came down, but only to say I couldn't have anything until Dr. Rutledge had been by—he was going to take my case, since I was from out of town. And, by the way, the police wanted to see me. After the doctor, I said. Another hour passed before Rutledge came by, a man in his late forties whose blond hair had lost none of its color.

"You're a very lucky man. A couple of inches down or back and those blows could have left you with serious broken bones or possibly even dead."

"That's cheering news," I rasped. After coughing again, I asked for water.

"Certainly."

"What about a fractured skull?"

"Again you were lucky. The X rays showed no fissures. You had a bad concussion, but you already seem better. And we didn't have to take any stitches. Do you feel up to seeing the police?"

I knew I would have to, so I said yes. I also knew I had to make up a story. Ever since the nurse had mentioned the police I knew I could not tell them what had really happened.

Rutledge went over to the boy's bed. Apparently he had injured a knee in football and was to have surgery. He might no longer be Saturday's hero—a tough break for an American kid. No wonder he was sulking. I let their conversation drift into the background, Rutledge's soothing voice reassuring the boy of his uncertain future, and thought of my own mistakes—how to cover and redeem them.

I should have lunged at Stedman rather than stepping back. Then I wouldn't be in a hospital bed and we'd all be on our way back to Cleveland. Returning Stedman to Bob would have finished the job. Let the police, let Carlson, deal with murder. Even a high fee wouldn't send me after that ten-year-old skeleton. But I didn't lunge; I protected myself defensively and nearly had my brain beaten in the effort. Now Stedman had to be found again; maybe even the skeleton would need to be identified. Old bones and broken bones. I laughed and found the other three staring at me.

As it turned out, telling the police a story wasn't difficult. I told them where I'd stopped and that I had been picked up by two men as I walked back from the diner. Apparently they'd

robbed me, but not before they'd knocked the hell out of me.
 The policemen were both in uniform, both wearing blue nylon parkas like the ones I had seen on the police in Green Hills. They were in their twenties. One with a moustache asked the questions; the younger, slighter of the two, took down my answers on a small pocket pad. He appeared uncomfortable at his task, as though words were rushing by too fast. When I mentioned robbery, they looked at me and at each other.
 The one with the moustache finally said, "There's over three hundred and fifty dollars in your wallet."
 Stedman hadn't even had sense enough to cover his path by making it seem like a robbery. Perhaps he'd thought there was no point in lying.
 "They must have been interrupted. Maybe another car came along."
 "Or maybe they were out for a little hell," put in the younger. I nodded and smiled ruefully. Pleased with my response to his suggestion, he smiled back.
 "I don't know why they didn't rob me. You'd have to ask them. If they're ever caught."
 We went on chatting quietly, going over the facts, my roommates listening—something hard to avoid. Then they asked me what I did. When I told them, they nodded. They'd seen my license.
 "Are you on a case?"
 "I was. But I finished it in New York, so I decided to do a little skiing. I like winter; why else would anyone walk when he could drive?"
 They looked uncertain but didn't press me. After a few more minutes they said they'd forward a report to the state police, but not to expect much, especially since I might not recognize my attackers. They left me with that modest reproach.
 I knew I had to leave. Eventually my lies could catch me, and the state police might send more thorough interrogators. I stood up and walked back and forth a few times, discovered I was tired but not dizzy, and decided I had to take a chance and leave. I went to the lavatory, then walked the hall several times. Same sense—tired, but not dizzy. The cast was a nuisance.

Rutledge had left for the morning. I signed myself out, wearing my torn shirt.

The next thing was to get to Exbridge. I found I still had the money the police had mentioned, so I got a cab to take me back to Exbridge and Mrs. Trumble's. It was expensive, but it gave me another chance to rest and didn't leave me the worse for wear.

Mrs. Trumble was worried about me, she said, and she looked it. I told her I'd had an accident while in a friend's car. I paid her for two days to keep her from pressing me and went upstairs for my things. I had to roll up the left sleeve of my shirt to get it on. Then I put the torn one in the suitcase and went downstairs. Mrs. Trumble was pacing at the foot of the steps. She was obviously curious and insisted on putting my suitcase in the car for me, probably convinced I was a gangster. In the rear view mirror she was standing at the end of her walk, her hands clasped before her abdomen, her energy keeping her warm.

It was about two when I stopped at the diner. Recognizing me, the owner said hello before he noticed the left sleeve hanging limp, the cast exposed before my coat.

"What happened?"

"Little accident in a friend's car. Let me have a couple more pork chops."

"You sure?" He looked doubtful.

"Yes, I can move these fingers." I lifted my arm and wiggled the fingers.

"Okay."

The coat rack was near the door. I walked back and hung up my coat with a minimum of trouble. What I wanted to see from the front of the diner was the hardware store across the street. No lights were visible, but there was a hand-lettered sign on white paper. I went back and sat down.

"What happened to the hardware store? It doesn't seem to be open."

"It's not. Paul called me last night. He's the fellow who owns the store. About eleven. Said his aunt died in Syracuse and they'd be leaving early today. I put that sign up for him. Funny,

I never knew he had an aunt, much less one whose funeral he'd go to."

"People can be strange about relatives."

"I suppose. I'm old enough that mine are all dead. Since I never married, I've got nobody to worry about." He turned the chops and they spattered loudly in the pan. "Course no one to care for me, either. Don't know what's best. Want some fried potatoes with these?"

"Sure." I didn't really care about the potatoes, but felt I owed him some agreeable company if I were picking his comments for my purpose. But he had little more to add. He hadn't seen Stedman since midafternoon the day before.

He cut the chops for me. I ate and left, heading back for Albany in the late afternoon. If I could get a flight that night I'd take it; if not, I could find a hotel room to wait until the next day. There was no point in going anywhere but home.

I was tired by the time I returned the rental car. The road over the mountains was even better than yesterday, but the dead weight of my left arm was tiring, and my right arm worked overtime for the curves. With some relief I learned I could get an evening flight. I checked my bag through.

While I had been in the hospital that morning I had decided to call Chris, to ask her to meet me. There were pay phones across from the ticket counters; with some real hesitation I got the operator to put the call through on my credit card number. Chris's phone rang three times before she said hello. Her voice was pleasant, soft, and I listened to its sound before responding.

"Chris." It seemed stupid to say nothing more, but after the way I'd last talked to her, anything might be stupid.

"Dave. I'm so glad you called." She paused. "I've been back for a week—ten days—and hadn't heard from you."

"I've been working."

"You sound tired."

"I am. How are you?"

"The same. I haven't given up on my music, after all."

"Good."

"I hoped you would be pleased."

"You knew I would be."

"Are you busy tonight? Or am I being too forward?"
"No—to both questions. Only I'm out of town."
"This is long distance?"
"I'm in Albany. Can you meet my plane—at eleven-thirty on American?"
"Sure. Are you okay?"
"Just tired. And tired of missing you."
"I love you."
How glad I was to hear that. "I love you."
"I'll be there." She hung up without saying good night.
I went out and found a seat in which to kill an hour. I slept most of the way back.

14

Chris was waiting on the other side of the inspection point. She had on a blue beret and the same blue leather coat she'd worn that day we'd met by the museum. She looked as fresh as if it were morning, not almost midnight. She had started toward me when she noted the small bandage on the side of my head and the accompanying bruises. She stopped, her smile fluttered, then she put her arms around my neck. I pressed her to me with my right arm and she felt the cast.

"Your arm, too. What's happened?"

Several people stared at us, but walked on.

"It's a long story, and I'm tired. Are you free?"

She simply nodded.

"Let's go to my place."

Again she nodded. We went down to claim my bag. Chris pulled closer to my right side. She took the suitcase when it came through and swiftly and skillfully guided me out to her car. She had me get in before she would put the bag in the trunk. I leaned back in the seat and closed my eyes. The next thing I knew she was sitting there in the driver's seat gently covering my left hand. When I looked over she smiled, then turned her face into the yellow lights and started the engine. We drove in silence to my apartment. After we were inside and she had hung up our coats and had taken my suitcase to the bedroom, she came out to find me in the kitchen.

"Would you like me to fix something to eat?"
"I just wanted some water."
"A drink?"
"Not even a drink. I can sleep without one."
"Then you should go to bed."

She guided me back, helped me undress and tucked me in. Somewhere in that time I asked her again if she was busy tomorrow. She shook her head, which was as much answer as I could recall. I was asleep before she turned out the light next to my bed.

I awoke at nine-thirty the next morning, Sunday. Chris was asleep beside me. I lay still, hoping not to disturb her and that I would go back to sleep. Neither wish was successful. I couldn't sleep. When I turned slightly, hoping to forget the weight of the cast so I might fall asleep, I woke Chris.

"Feeling any better?"

I nodded. "Did you sleep well?"

"Pretty well. I had a hard time going to sleep. I was worried about you." There was no self-pity or dominance, only a simple statement of fact. We were both on our backs with the covers up to our chins, the thermostat turned down. I felt her bare leg against mine.

"You looked pretty bad last night. Care to tell me about it?"

"Sure, after I get another drink of water."

I went to the bathroom for the water. When I came back she was getting back into bed after opening the curtain onto the balcony. The apartment was on the fifteenth floor, and the bedroom faced the lake. We pressed against each other. I put my right arm around her shoulders and she let her head rest on me.

"Are you sure this doesn't hurt?"

"I'm much better. Only the cast is a nuisance now."

"How long do you have to have it on?"

I laughed. "I forgot to ask and no one said. I'll go see someone here, in a few days. How have you been?"

"Not bad." She paused. "I'm glad you called last night."

"I'm glad you said what you did."

"What was that?"

"That you love me."

"I am too." She rubbed her head back and forth over my shoulder.

"How was the tour?"

"Okay. A couple of state universities, a couple of liberal arts colleges. Jake almost wouldn't go on one night." Thinking of the event amused her.

"What was wrong?"

"The audience—all twenty-five or thirty of them. You should have seen him sputter. 'Twenty-five thousand students, and this . . . where is the faculty . . . intellectually dead . . . dead.' We convinced him not to punish those who did show up. I think it may have been our best performance of the tour."

"I thought Jake complained about the phonies who would fill an auditorium."

"He does." She laughed, nodding her head on my chest. "He hates the standing ovation—'They don't understand anything. The dummies. . . . ' "

"I wish I'd gone with you."

"Do you?"

"Yes. I think I was being foolish. I was."

"I wish we didn't have so much to catch up on."

"Are you leaving again?"

"Not for a while. After the semester starts. But I meant . . . I only wish we could live now and not have to summarize the past for each other."

"Can you stay today?"

"Not the whole day. We have a rehearsal at two. But I can come back tonight."

"Good. We'll need that time to make up for the time we spend summarizing."

"Are you going to tell me what happened to you?"

"It's a long story."

"I listen well."

"Let's not do that now."

She raised her head and we kissed. "How are you going to manage with that?" She tapped the cast with her nail.

"Roll over on top of me."

She did, and instead of a hot, clear sky over us, there was a dull gray one, almost as smooth from corner to corner of the window as a blanket on a well-made bed. I held her to me with my right arm, and once she asked me how my arm was, but I simply gave a slight nod.

She showered while I shaved, and when I took a bath she washed my back and right arm as I hung the left arm over the side of the tub. Afterwards we each found a robe and went out to the kitchen.

"What do you want to eat?" she asked.

"Anything."

"Eggs?"

"An omelet."

She grimaced. "You tell me what to do."

After several minutes chopping and a couple cooking we turned out two western omelets. The problem was that I ordinarily cooked breakfast for us, so I had to give her directions.

We were both hungry and did little talking. Then, over a second cup of instant coffee, she asked, "Did you mean that about wishing you had gone with me?"

"Yes."

"I hope it isn't because of your arm that you wish that."

"It's not. You've been back two weeks. I . . . "

"Yet you didn't call." She was puzzled, not angry.

"I came by one night, a couple of days ago. The lights were out. I've changed in the last two weeks. I don't think the same way any longer, not about us."

"Is that good?"

"I think so. We'll see."

She didn't press me. "You never did tell me what happened to your arm."

"A man with an axe handle tried to kill me. At least I think he wanted me dead. Without beating me to death, he left me to die." I told her the whole story from beginning to end. She already knew about the skeleton from the newspaper. When I finally had the whole story out our coffee cups were empty and cold.

"Do you want anything more?" She reached out and covered my right hand with her left. I shook my head.

"What bothers me is the discovery that my cynical attitude should be true. I told you I couldn't trust anyone. That you were the first person I'd trusted in three years." I paused and looked at her eyes; she pressed my hand. "In the back of my mind was the unstated feeling that there are rules and that every once in a while you find someone to trust—not to love. That somehow we have to rely on trust to make things work. And that I have to believe that every once in a while someone is telling me the truth. In waiting for that somebody, I have to take on trust what I can't absolutely disprove."

"It's not really trust, is it?"

"No. You can say it's distrust; taking on distrust until I can disprove the view. But they're opposite sides of a coin. I knew, or thought I did, that my attitude was cynical—don't count on anyone. And I thought I was getting away from some of the obvious manipulation of the truth by certain preordained rules when I left the law. That seemed to me the height of cynicism—to claim to establish order by a fixed plan that seldom allowed any establishment of truth. But I was blind. I've been an idealist playing cynic, and I've played badly."

"I knew you were an idealist all along. Why else would I love you, too?" She smiled as she pursed her lips.

"What of all that talk of my independence?"

"That"—she smiled—"was my own self-pity. You remembered." She tipped her head on her left hand. "I knew your money was behind your independence. There's nothing wrong with using your opportunities. It's a lot better to try and to miss than to sit on your tail counting your money."

"Okay."

"Yes. No sense in self-punishment over something you didn't create. But you're not so simple as to tell me that because you got a broken arm you now know for certain that you can't trust anyone."

"In a way. Stedman may have attacked me only because he didn't trust me. He and I may have shared more in attitudes than I ever realized. He had built a new world, a new identity, cutting himself off from the past, which meant he distrusted everything outside of his new world. Haven't I done something similar?"

She didn't say anything at first, and I realized we were thinking the same thing. "But you didn't kill anyone." I nodded as she spoke.

"He may not have, either. But he was hiding from some terrible fears—a neglected son, three dead men."

"So how big was his world that you intruded on?"

"As large as mine—one woman."

"Not even his store, that little town?"

"No. Anyone could come in, as I did, and carry the past in with him."

"So he lived in fear."

"And that's what he showed me. He is just the extreme example of an attitude I have, and that most people have to a lesser degree. Only a few stupid idealists are so troglodytic as to believe in truth."

"A primitive man?" She laughed. "You are being hard on yourself."

"No, no. Only a primitive hermit. Maybe I should become one."

"Don't desert me when you desert the world."

"I won't."

"It's not very pleasant to think of how frightened and alone most of us are."

"It's not. And I know I invade that fear each time I talk to someone. God, I'm tired. The distrust and dishonesty . . . what's the use?"

"We need idealists."

"And what of the artists?"

She laughed. "No one is more idealistic. I feel very compatible with you."

"What of our independence?"

"We can still have it. I respect you and myself too much to give it up." Her eyes were moist enough to sparkle.

"I'm glad I called you—and that you were home."

"Where else?" Then she looked at me seriously. "Can your

idealism take the fact that your cynical approach was right all along?"

"Yes. I shouldn't tell you this, but I learned to live with it yesterday. But it helped to get it out."

"To me?"

"To you." I nodded.

"What are you going to do now? It's twelve-thirty. I'm going to have to leave."

"I think I'll sit out one more day. Frankly, I don't know where to go unless Stedman shows up, and I'm too tired for Carlson or the Larches. Would you make a couple of phone calls before you go?"

"Sure."

"Call Mary. I want to know if anyone has been by to ask for me. Then call the Larches and ask for Robert Stedman. I'll tell you what to say. Don't let Mary know I'm back in town."

She went over to the phone and called Mary, who was obviously surprised to learn that I had called Chris. It was clear someone had been by, from the length of time Chris was on the phone. When she hung up she looked at me knowingly.

"You expected someone, didn't you?"

"Yes."

"Carlson called."

"And someone else?"

"Yes. Robert Stedman was there day before yesterday, the same day Carlson was also looking for you."

"That's strange; he's been gone from his house since the day after he hired me. I have a feeling he's going to fire me."

"Why would he do that?"

"I'm not sure. That can of worms he enjoyed opening on his family may have become his own snakepit. He's not a bad kid, but he's had no support, probably no love, for ten years, maybe for all twenty-one."

"Do you think he's beyond help?"

"No. But anything I do may be damaging."

"And he knows that intuitively?"

I shook my head, smiling. "I don't know."

"What shall I say when I call him?"

149

"I've changed my mind. Call my answering service for me. I don't care who else was calling, so tell them I expected a call from Bob. Better tell her you're my secretary."

This call was more formal, to the point where I wondered if Chris would get the information I wanted. But she knew to say she worked for Mary and to use her own name so Mary would know if the service checked. When she put the phone down she was smiling.

"I was good, wasn't I?"

"Depends on what you learned."

She came over and put her arms around my neck.

"Robert Stedman called this morning, three times yesterday, twice the day before. He's anxious to talk."

"He'll have to wait until tomorrow."

"I can't wait any longer. I can't be late. Come on back while I dress."

She brushed her hair, dressed and put on a little makeup in less than ten minutes, talking all the time.

"Why are you going to make him wait?"

"Because I don't want him to fire me. I'm hoping his father will show up. If he does, I want to be there."

"What makes you think he'll be there by tomorrow?"

"I don't expect him; I'm biding my time."

"Why did you have me make those calls?" She put down the brush and turned from the mirror.

"Now you're the only one who has talked to me. That keeps Carlson or Bob one step away."

"So I take the responsibility." She walked to the closet.

"I hope not, but I know you can if it should happen to come your way."

She said nothing for a few seconds. When she came back she was pulling a dress down over her hips. "Zip me up. I hope I don't have to."

I pulled up the zipper but couldn't hook her dress. An awkward job with one hand. "Don't worry. If anyone should come by this afternoon, play the indignant artist and make them wait."

She laughed at the idea. "Do policemen fall for that?"

"Probably not. But you have to learn to stall."

"You seem very good at that." I knew what she meant.

"Are you coming back tonight?"

"Yes." Her sudden direct simplicity caught me by surprise. I could only say, "Good." It was all I felt.

"Now I really have to go." She turned away and went to the front hall closet.

"If you need to call me, ring twice, hang up and call again."

"Dramatic." She lifted the ends of her hair above her coat collar.

"Yes. Get something for dinner."

"What?"

"Anything. Let's celebrate."

"Us?"

"Yes."

She closed the door. I went out to the kitchen, rinsed the dishes and put them in the dishwasher. The arm hurt some, so I lay down. I kept wondering if I was right about Bob Stedman. I couldn't take the chance that I wasn't, because without a client Carlson would have me run in for driving by the Larch place. I felt sorry for the kid, because even the father he now allowed himself to think of had deserted him. He never really had placed his son high on his priorities; I had learned that from his own mouth two days earlier. Nothing was higher than his own security, and I had the arm to prove it. I had to quit thinking about what was done, so I got a copy of Trevelyan on nineteenth-century England, thinking that was as far from what I was now doing as I needed to be. After twenty pages I fell asleep.

At about three forty-five the doorbell rang. The noise was indistinct and unidentifiable for several seconds. When I realized the source of the ringing I lay still, the book on my chest. It had to be either Bob or Carlson, and I finally decided to get my meeting with one of them over. It was neither.

By the time I reached the door Leslie had given up and was on her way to the elevator. She had heard my door and stopped, facing a wall as though undecided which way to go.

"Mrs. Larch."

"I'm sorry I woke you, Mr. Stuart." She smiled formally, without warmth. "I had no idea you would be asleep at this hour." She came back to my door.

Since her mother-in-law was paying Bob's bills, including mine, I was nettled by her apparent condescension. "I got in late last night. And"—I held up my arm—"I'm a little the worse for wear."

"My goodness." An innocuous expression, but well meant, by her tone of voice. "How did that happen?"

"A careless accident."

She knew I didn't want to say more about it, so she asked no more. Her tone had changed, and I realized she had not meant her behavior to be interpreted as I had. As I watched her I realized she was nervous, not hostile.

"Come in, won't you?" We were still standing by the door. I smiled. "Before neighbors' tongues wag."

"Are you sure I won't be disturbing you?"

There was no sarcasm in her voice. On the contrary, I thought I heard a sense of hope.

"No. Please come in. Go on in and sit down, won't you? I think it's time I got dressed. Can I get you anything while you wait?"

She shook her head. "No, thank you."

"How did you know I was home?"

She frowned. "It never occurred to me that you wouldn't be. I went to your office, and since you weren't there I came over here. I was blindly, thoughtlessly wishing."

I nodded and left her standing by the living room window and went to change. I felt I was fast, considering, and managed to leave only my left cuff unbuttoned around the cast. Whatever she wanted to say couldn't wait; otherwise she wouldn't be at my door in the middle of Sunday afternoon.

When I returned to the living room she was still standing by the window.

"Sorry to keep you. Won't you sit down?"

"Of course. This is a very nice view. Too bad the lake isn't in better shape, but the view of the lights must be grand."

"On those few clear nights we have."

She sat by the window, allowing herself a way to avoid me by looking out the window.

"I wondered if you had seen Bob yet."

"You came to see me for him?"

I must have sounded skeptical, because her voice quavered for a moment.

"Yes . . . of course. He . . . he's very upset, and I'm the only one who listens to him. Ben has only the slightest of sympathies. I'm not even sure it is sympathy. And Bob's mother is withdrawing into herself over this; I suppose I can understand why."

"The obvious reasons," I said.

"You mean for her withdrawal?" I nodded my response. "Yes, of course."

"So he talked to you?"

"He came down to the house looking for Ben. That was two days ago. I was the only one home. He just started pouring it out. He is terribly confused."

She now ignored the window, the city spread out before us, the gray sky. She watched me with an earnestness that revealed her need to help him, and twisted the strap of her purse in her fingers.

"Did he say where he's been?"

"With friends, acquaintances, I don't know. He was on drugs."

"How do you know?"

"He told me. He said he was depressed and they helped him, but he looked tired to me."

"Probably from amphetamines. He could be feeling the letdown when he talked to you. Did he tell you why he was depressed?"

"The body, of course."

"I mean specifically. Does he know more than he's told me? More than the letter?"

"I don't think so. He's afraid of you and what you'll find. He doesn't want the truth now. One minute he would talk of how his father was dead; the next he wondered if his father wasn't a murderer. I told him to see you, but I didn't know you were away when I told him that."

"Are you going back there now?"

"I'm not going back."

I tried not to show my surprise, for even if she and Ben weren't close, there was no sign of separation looming. "Your decision?"

"Yes. That's why I came to see you." She smiled in a desperately friendly way. "When I'm gone, I'm afraid of what Bob may do."

"Would you call him for me?"

"No. I don't want to take a chance on getting Ben, or his mother." Her voice was firm.

"I'd like to wait until tomorrow. In case he blames me still."

"I understand. Do what you think is best."

"This was sudden." I let my words hang between observation and question.

She didn't need to answer me, and if she had become angry I wouldn't have been surprised, since most people don't want to talk of divorce or separation while it occurs. But she must have needed to talk, or believed it was relevant to Bob's needs. If the latter was true I had to respect her self-renunciation.

"You saw us this week, but the problem is not new."

"You mean I saw your husband's anger over your dogs."

"Yes. What you saw was a symptom, not a cause."

My memory went back to our first encounter when she left the room, an action her mother-in-law remarked upon as sensitivity, as though some of life were too much for Leslie. Or Ben's original praise of her dogs. But dogs and animal ways, breeding them, hardly seemed appropriate to a woman who found life too much. Perhaps Ben's praise was cosmetic, to make me believe life was better than it seemed. But her husband and mother-in-law could care for her, admiring the very qualities they praised.

If she weren't so attractive and direct, or apparently direct, I doubted that I would be so inclined to believe her. Perhaps I only wanted to believe her right. I thought I might not have cared who was telling the truth in this instance if the whole family weren't connected in varying, as yet undetermined, ways with that skeleton.

"What's it a symptom of?"

"There is much more wrong than my dogs. I enjoy them, but they don't mean that much to me. I'd sell them now if Ben wanted me to. Sometimes I wish he would, but he never will. You must see why."

"I do. You said the car was his baby. But can't you share his art, if not your dogs?"

"His art." She smiled and shook her head. "I really feel strange going on like this. It's not your business, and it's not going to help Bob, who is the reason I came to see you." She stood up, but went to the window, not the door.

I seriously wondered if Bob was the reason she had come, if she wasn't deluding herself.

"There isn't any art in what he's doing. I feel sorry for Ben; his ability is in sales. That's what he does, not art. His mother is the one with the taste and buying judgment. If it weren't for those abilities, even more than her money, he would still be working for Inter-Lake. He goes to those auctions with her identity."

I saw the two of them at the desk, going over catalogues. It was possible she was telling him what to buy, making the only and final decisions.

"You mean it's a charade they play?"

"I suppose so. I never thought of it that way. But it is a game where one action stands for another. She is a very bright, industrious woman." She gave a slight laugh and turned back to me. "In another decade she might have been free—a liberated woman."

"She has a very damaged life that you're forgetting."

"No. How could I forget it this week? And if you'll believe me, it would be hard to forget, living as close to her as we have. That's probably one of the reasons I feel so sorry for Bob. Someone from there deserves a chance."

"What are you going to do?"

"Go home to Mommy and Daddy." She smiled wanly.

"Where's that?"

"Detroit. He's a surgeon—successful—though not like Ben's family."

"Then?"

"I have to think it over. I doubt if we can repair ourselves. We're too old. Too settled, trapped."

I agreed they were trapped, but not by age; but I wouldn't tell her.

"I lack Mrs. Larch's stamina, her spunk, her . . . whatever. She went on after being deserted. I'm the deserter."

"Such comparisons are inaccurate."

"And odious?"

I nodded.

"Well, I had better go. I won't be home until late this evening, and they don't expect me. You will try to help Bob. Don't let him come apart, too. We're not the tidiest of families, and this is a particularly messy time."

"I'll see him. I'm glad you came by. I'd better know before I get there: did you leave your husband a note?"

"Yes. I doubt if he's surprised."

"I didn't want to be the one to tell him."

"I wouldn't do that to you. Thank you for listening." She came forward with her hand extended.

"Drive carefully. Is that sky going to drop more snow on us?"

She looked at it again, even though she had just come from the window. "I don't know."

"Never mind. Talking about the weather is what people do when they meet, not when they say good-by." Then, for only a moment, she looked tired, not simply controlled as I had once seen her. The self-restraint had worn her down, and not merely over the last few days.

We simply said good-by and I let her out. I didn't watch her go to the elevator. Perhaps what she'd said was right: Marian Larch was stronger than most people. Certainly Bolen thought so. I wondered how she would be about this. Her feelings might be more important than Ben's.

15

Chris came in at seven, all smiles, with her right arm around a bag of groceries and a red scarf wrapped around her head and draped behind her neck.

"Where's your beret?"

"In the car. This feels more like the celebration we're going to have. I brought you something." She set the bag on the counter by the refrigerator. Unhooking her purse from her left arm, she opened it.

"Here. What no working hero should be without."

It was a black sling.

"I don't feel very heroic, and if you don't mind my saying so, that's not going to make me look very heroic."

"Here, try it on." She smiled with pleasure at my limitation as she put the sling around my neck.

"You're enjoying this."

"How often have I had a chance to take care of you?"

"Never."

"That's right. If you thought I was going to dominate you . . ."

"If you could."

"Would . . . never. I'm being protective of you. How does it fit?" She stepped back.

"Like a sling."

"You look handsome. I can see you already with a suit coat

thrown over your shoulder." She put her right elbow on the counter and placed her hand on her chin, her fingers over her mouth, looking up at me. I could see the smile forming as her lips pulled away from her fingers.

"How about buying me a small-caliber gun to carry in it?"

She laughed. Her arms went around my back, the cast separating us.

"As you see, I won't be able to wear it in bed."

"Why not?" Her face was pressed against my right shoulder.

"I suppose I might. Under certain circumstances."

"But not tonight."

"I thought you wanted me to try it right away."

"Only during daylight hours."

"I'm glad that's settled. Now you can get on to more important matters, such as what you bought for our celebration."

She tapped my right shoulder blade and backed away. "Veal—we're going to have scallopini."

"Anything I can do?"

"Fix us a drink while I clean the mushrooms."

I mixed her a rum gimlet, then poured some Scotch over ice for myself. By the time I was seated at the kitchen table, she was finished with the mushrooms.

"Beautiful veal, but it ought to be, for the price." She began pounding it. Chris knew as well as I where everything was in the kitchen.

"Leslie Larch was here while you were gone."

"Was she?" She gave the last piece of veal a couple of whacks.

"She wants me to look out for Bob."

"And she felt it was necessary to come over to tell you?" The fragrance of olive oil filled the air. She dropped the meat into a paper bag holding seasoned flour.

"No. She felt it was necessary to see me to tell me she was leaving her husband."

"Not much stamina in a time of crisis. Or do you think she knows something else?"

"I doubt it." I told her what I'd seen of the distance Leslie experienced in the family.

"And you think she's been that way for some time." Chris wiped her hands and sipped her drink.

"I don't know, but it's logical to think so." I looked at her, hoping she would respond, but she was cooking the mushrooms. "It's probable that she has, because that's a house of loners."

The mushrooms sputtered; she stirred them.

"Isn't that the common element in all the people you told me about?" She picked up her glass. "The man you followed—Stedman—he left the house ten years ago. Leslie is leaving her husband now, and the kid who hired you is on drugs."

"Exactly. Except for two people, there are no permanent residents."

"You think one of them is a murderer?" She drank from her glass, then put it down in order to take the mushrooms from the pan and add the meat. "Here, Dave, make yourself helpful again and fix a salad."

"How am I going to do that?"

"Rinse the lettuce, hold it on the counter with your left hand, and tear it into pieces."

"Where's your compassion?" I asked as I stood up, taking a long swallow of Scotch. She turned away to ignore me by putting rolls in the oven.

"No, I don't know," I said as I stood over the sink. "Stedman could easily be the murderer. Frankly, without a confession, I think that murder is unsolvable."

"Here are some bowls. Then why don't you simply resign from the case? Why worry about whether Bob fires you or not?"

"I want to know."

"There you go again."

"Not very fast with this lettuce."

"Take the meat out of the pan while I do your job."

"Do you want any wine in the drippings?"

"Yes."

"Do you want me to quit?" I asked as I went to the refrigerator.

"Of course. A broken arm and a concussion are enough."

"More than enough, but they didn't give me any answers."

"What do you hope for?"

"Stedman's reappearance." It was possible, depending on why he had hit me, or how he thought of what he had done. If compassion for his son or a sense of responsibility for three dead men could be strong enough, he might reappear in Cleveland. On the other hand, if he were frightened at being discovered, or by his attack on me, he might run forever.

I had one other hope, too, that Leslie's departure might trigger a break in the unity of Ben Larch and his mother.

16

The next morning I gave Al Burke a call at his office to tell him about Frank Ashe. He was ready to be angry with me for not answering my phone a few nights before, but he stopped to let me talk about Ashe. I had no proof and had lost the one witness I'd had, but I thought the police might as well keep him in mind.

They had. Al asked me to wait and called back ten minutes later. Ashe had died two years before in an attempted holdup. A gas station attendant had shot him. He had been a known junkie, apparently out to fix a habit.

"Why did he need to hold up a gas station? His share of the savings and loan robbery should have been a quarter of a million."

"The money has never shown up. Maybe it never will."

"That doesn't make any sense. A junkie won't sit on that kind of money."

"Maybe the murders frightened them off."

"You know the murders were a part of the plan."

"You sound awfully certain." He was more amused than irritated.

"I read the newspaper account this last week. Those three guards were killed outright so they couldn't interfere."

"Then two more men know. We'll have the police start checking Ashe's file. Thanks for the tip."

"Sorry it was too late to help you."

We hung up.

It made no more sense of the situation than before that three-quarters of a million dollars should disappear without a trace. A fence would have taken it at the poorest rate of exchange. And he wouldn't have held the money this long.

I left Chris, telling her I would come to her place that night.

The sun came out, for the first time in days, when I was about a mile from Larches. I was relieved of the thought of leaving town to find the sun. Smog and smoke had not blotted out the sky, not permanently yet. Through the woods the trees made long shadows, and the trunks that had seemed gray took on a variety of tones and shades. The white house at the hilltop glistened in the sun.

The same maid opened the door, casting a doubtful eye on me. When I asked for Bob Stedman she was visibly relieved, allowing her mouth to curve up. Rather than telling me to wait, and without taking my topcoat, she led the way back to the kitchen, down the hall, past the library and to the right. Bob was sitting in an alcove, wiping a plate of its yellow remnants with a last corner of toast, while waiting for another piece to pop up for him.

"Stuart, sit down. Did your answering service tell you I'd been trying to reach you?"

The maid had gone to the sink for some invisible task, and before I could answer he looked past me and spoke sharply to her. "Charlene, you can come back later."

She said nothing, jammed the faucet shut and walked out. He waited until we could no longer hear her footsteps before speaking.

"Sit down. I trust you've spent my money well."

I told myself he needed patience, but I couldn't make myself easy on him. Disappointed at my own lack of success, I cut loose on him.

"Let's get something straight. When you hired me, you paid for one day. Since then your mother has given me five hundred for expenses, and that went for airplane tickets and hospital expenses. This bandage, these bruises and this arm were done on my time. So pay up or cut the crap."

Coming on like an eighteenth-century lord suited neither the situation nor him. I sat down without being asked, irritated because I had come to do him a service, with no certainty I'd be paid. I'd seen people with money become huffy to avoid paying, and knew he could pull the same stunt. But I figured this was his way of steeling himself to fire me. Then he backed off.

"How much do I owe you?" He wouldn't apologize, but he would meet his present responsibility.

"Twelve hundred more, plus two more days in advance. No charge for Sunday."

Without asking why, and certainly without humor, he said, "I'll get you a check."

"Eat your toast." It sat cooling in the toaster. "Let me guess why you feel so chipper."

"What do you mean?" He looked away to take the toast and laid it on his plate.

"Your sister-in-law left yesterday, and right now you're feeling superior."

"Why shouldn't I? Somebody else finally wised up to Ben." He spit the words, then turned and jabbed his knife into the butter.

"So you feel better."

"You're damned right."

"Have you thought about why?"

"I already told you."

"What about your new sense of superiority? Ben has been brought low."

"So what?"

"Are you really satisfied that you can condescend to him, the way you've been condescended to?"

"Yes." His voice was high and sharp. His fist holding the butter-covered knife was on the table, the knife erect. Without moving he gave a feebler, "Yes."

"I thought you were better than this. Don't you want to know how I knew Leslie was gone?"

For a few seconds he did nothing. Finally he nodded.

"She asked me to be sure you were okay. Before she left

town yesterday she came to see me, mainly because of you."

"Did she really?" He set the knife down and looked at me.

"Yes. She's been worried about you. Where you'd gone, whom you'd been with."

"I didn't know."

"Of course not; you've been too stuck on yourself, or else hiding."

"Did she tell you I've been on pills?"

"Yes. I also think she knew you were asking for help."

"She's better than Ben deserved."

"How about you?"

"I deserved a break."

"Cut it out. I thought for a few seconds you were wising up. You may not have had it easy, but if you keep bitching about it you'll never have it better."

"Will you tell me what you learned if I pay you?"

I sighed. "I came here to tell you anyway."

"I will pay you—first."

He got up and left the room. The remaining egg yolk had congealed on his plate. Oils floated on his cold coffee. He'd almost come out and then he'd failed. I'd come on hard, but I wouldn't blame myself, because he'd proved often enough that he was fouled up.

"Here." He held the check out to me. "It's good, even if it is on my account. My mother keeps me in money." His tone indicated embarrassment. She probably provided little else. He sat down again.

I folded it and put it into my inside suit pocket.

"Now, what did you learn . . . for that?" He was picking up the family values.

"Your father is alive."

He almost smiled. At first the eyebrows rose and the mouth dropped in surprise; then he tried to mask his shock with pleasure; then all feeling disappeared.

"Where did you see him?"

"In a small Massachusetts town, Exbridge."

"You saw him?"

"Yes. In a hardware store he owns."

"Is he coming back here?"

"I don't know."

"Why not?"

"Because he gave me these before he left me to die in a woods."

Showing no shock or concern he went on, "Did you tell him about me? That I'd hired you?"

"Yes."

"He'll be back. He will."

"Perhaps." Suddenly I was sorry I'd been so angry.

"No, he will." Passionate intensity overrode any possible exception. "I know he will. I deserve that much."

"You know he may be a murderer."

"What do you mean?" Doubt clouded his intense gaze.

"The skeleton. If it isn't his, did he put it there?"

"No."

"We talked about this the day you hired me."

"I remember. I'm not a child. But he couldn't do that. Not the man . . . the man in the picture."

The picture had become a permanent reality.

"He saw three men die, knew who did the killing, and never told the police."

"What are you talking about?"

"After you had disappeared earlier this week, I learned there was a robbery where three men died, right outside his store. He knew one of the killers." I hesitated, watching him reject each statement I made. "While we're on that story, he ran off with his partner's wife, deserting your mother . . . and you."

"Not me, her. How can anyone live here? I can't stand it."

"You take the money."

He hesitated; his hand went to his chin. "Why shouldn't I?" He stood up and walked to the sink, seizing the stainless steel edge. "Why the hell shouldn't I?"

"Ordinarily I would agree. But you're tearing yourself up by taking your family's money. You depend on your mother for support, while you take your father's side. You know she's not all to blame."

"Not even for not loving me, for putting me in a second-class position because she hates my father? She hates him enough to kill—you talk about killers." His eyes squinted as he turned from staring at the sunlight.

She could, I thought. But my problem now was Bob. "I'm not trying to quarrel with you. On the contrary, you do deserve a break. But you're not getting it by entering your parents' quarrel."

"I'm already there."

"Maybe, but you don't need to push yourself in deeper."

"I must." He shook his head, then started out of the kitchen. "I'm going to tell Ben my father is coming back."

"But you don't know that."

"Yes, I do. Besides, you wanted me to act. Well, I'm going to do something positive."

He'd taken what I'd meant about his mental state and applied it to physical action. I followed him. In the front hall, throwing his green parka on, he was on his way to the door.

"Where is Ben?"

"Up by the lake."

"Where?"

"At some property we own."

"I'll drive you. My car is out front."

"To keep me out of trouble?" He went out the door.

"If need be." I shouted, "Get in!" I pointed to my car.

He did as I said. I turned over the engine, took a look at him, from which I learned nothing, and started down the hill. He said nothing, tapping a finger on his legs. I turned right and headed north.

After a couple of miles he said, "Go up to the lake and turn east."

From then on, until we reached a fenced-in wooded area on the north side of the road, he said nothing. As the moments of silence built up I was convinced I was right to watch him. Leslie was right about his needing help. Finally he told me to turn into a drive blocked by a chain with a no trespassing sign hanging from it. I stopped against the chain. Before I pulled to a full halt, his door opened and he was out, unhooking the chain. He said nothing when he was back in. I eased across the chain and stopped.

"Do you want to hook the chain?"

"Why bother? Go on."

The road was over level ground. The coarse gravel pavement led through a couple of curves to an open field on a low bluff overlooking the lake.

At the opposite edge of the field, about one hundred yards away, Ben Larch was swinging a shotgun in skeet-shooting fashion. No shots were fired. To his right stood a one-hundred-foot oak tree, silent survivor of countless changes. The red MG was on the other side of the tree.

No sooner had he come into sight than Bob said, "Stop here."

I turned off the engine and waited for Bob to move, but for a full thirty seconds he only stared. Then, just as suddenly, he opened the door, stepped out and slammed the door behind him, hard.

My eyes turned from him to the figure across the field. Ben had wheeled about when the door slammed. His shotgun, still at his shoulder, aimed at us. Like his half-brother, he too allowed our presence to sink in before he moved. Slowly he lowered the gun and turned around. He appeared to break the gun, removing the shells to replace them in his pocket.

Bob started across the stubble of the field. I got out and followed, in a stiff wind. Ben had walked away from us to the edge of the bluff, then started in the direction of his car, only to stop. Bob moved steadily, as though he knew what he wanted to do and was determined to act according to his plan. How rational, or safe, he might be was indeterminable. Ben's actions, equally unintelligible, revealed the uncertainty that preceded decision. I was only a spectator, a particularly helpless one, too. Before I would have wished it, they were face to face.

"I hadn't expected to be interrupted." Ben's face was grim. He pulled up the collar of an expensive brown wool shooting jacket.

"It is cold." Bob hugged himself. "You must have been thinking of Leslie."

The red cold disappeared for a moment from Ben Larch's

cheeks. He choked back his anger, his eyes flashing; then he glanced at me before looking at his brother. "Yes, that's right." He was just short of open rage.

"You need some help with the hand trap?"

"No . . . I . . . all right, if you want to. I'm out of practice."

Bob picked up the hand trap, inserting the clay bird. "Are you ready?"

"No, I unloaded the gun."

I'd been right. He took two shells from his right pocket, placing them in the still broken gun, and snapped it shut. He put the gun to his shoulder.

Before Ben said anything, Bob swung, releasing the bird at a high angle. Ben, following it, fired. The bird disappeared in a cloud of blue dust, and the report echoed back from the trees. Bob put another bird in, swung this time nearly directly level with his chest. Again the explosion, dust and echo. Only this time, because of the low angle, we saw the red spot on the ice below us. It was out about twenty yards, beyond the distance at which the birds had disappeared in blue puffs. It was what was left of a common gull, waiting to be scavenged by any animal that might find it, or to disappear during a thaw.

"I see you didn't need my help. Does that make three for three?"

Ben said nothing, removing the shells and dropping them into his left pocket. I had a feeling his demonstration of proficiency was meant to prove his calm condition. He would not be goaded into breaking down.

"May I try it?" asked Bob. His face was clear of expression. No sarcasm, no guile.

"You've never shot before." He turned to me. "Perhaps Mr. Stuart should be our guest."

"Hadn't you noticed his broken arm?" Bob spoke up before I could answer.

Ben glanced at him momentarily, then looked to me for confirmation. He saw the cast protruding from my coat, unprotected by the leather gloves I had foolishly forgotten to replace with wool.

"How did it happen?"

"An accident." I tried unsuccessfully to forestall conversation on the matter.

"My father broke it."

Ben started to turn but held himself back and looked at me. "Is that so?"

"Yes."

"Where is he?"

"I don't know," I said.

"Coming back here." Bob was convinced.

"Now why would he do that after attacking Mr. Stuart?"

"To see me."

Wisely, Ben said nothing. He took a deep breath. The color had returned to his face.

"I'm sorry about what happened, Mr. Stuart." Bob started to speak but stopped as Ben went on. "Give it a try, Bob." He turned, putting two new shells in before handing the gun over. He gave some basic instructions as he loaded the hand trap. He swung at a slight angle, a fairly easy shot directly in front of Bob.

The gun exploded and echoed, but the bird sailed on, shattering on the ice. Bob shifted his feet uneasily but said nothing. None of us did. Ben looked over to see if the gun was on his shoulder, then swung. The second bird took almost the same path as the first. Again Bob missed and the bird smashed on the ice.

Bob broke the gun, then dropped the shells on the crust of snow.

"I've not had your luck."

"Or training."

"Or advantages."

"I'll be glad to help you if you want some advice."

The advantage had swung to Ben. Bob's erratic behavior put Leslie's departure in the background and obscured Ben's reaction to it. Now he was the helpful older brother, troubled only by a petulant sibling.

"Help me? Like that gull?" Bob let his right hand swing toward the lake.

"That was bad judgment. You know I'm upset."

"How do you feel about seeing your stepfather?" Bob asked.

Ben ran his tongue behind his lips and tipped his head to one side in a mild shrug. "I'm pleased for you." He put his right hand into the pocket that held the shells.

"Jesus. You lying bastard. What have you ever cared about me? For ten years you crapped all over me every time you mentioned him. Remember, he's the weasel. Finally . . . finally our mother did something, got you to stop. I've been alone all that time. Even in day school my classmates knew . . . five years later."

"What was I supposed to do? You and I weren't close in age."

"I don't know, but you never did it."

"I've got enough on my mind today without this goddam maudlin remembrance of things past."

"Shit. It's no more maudlin than your self-pity over Leslie. You go right out and shoot some sea gull. I lived for ten years. You self-righteous hypocrite. You and Mother—the perfect pair—turned off and tuned out for ten rotten years."

"Don't you drag her into this. I've tried to keep calm until now." His chest moved quickly.

"Calm is what you've always been. Or else you and she ignored me together."

"I said not to discuss her. She married that nonentity and gave him a chance. And he deserted her." His voice rose to a shout of rage in the last sentence.

Bob's knuckles were white on the barrel and stock of the gun.

"This has gone far enough," I said as I started past Ben to take the gun.

"Nonentity, you bastard." Bob's hands shifted as he swung the broken gun at me at waist height. I fell backward to avoid being hit, coming down on my right arm. Unable to control my left side, I rolled onto it with almost full weight. I heard the gun smash against the tree as I fell. The crunching, shattering sounds continued as I rolled, and for a moment I thought I had been there before. I got to my knees, then stood up in time to see Ben break from a stupor to lunge at Bob. He didn't know what he was doing, because the splintered, twisted remains caught him in the side on the backswing. Bob finished the swing, struck again, and then turned to us. He was panting, with beads of perspiration on his upper lip and forehead, just where they were the first day I had seen him.

Standing there among the vanquished, there was no smile on Bob's face, no victory, and I was glad, for as I looked between the two men I knew it was a pyrrhic victory at best. Ben lay on the ground holding his side, writhing dramatically, making no sound. I pressed my left arm to my side, with the aid of my right, in an unnecessary attempt to protect it.

Bob dropped what remained of the shotgun, swept his forearm across his face. Not more than a minute had passed and we were all as devastated as the gun. He looked at each of us, expressionlessly, then ran to the MG. He turned over the engine and made a wild, almost uncontrolled arc as he backed it around to face the road. The gears jammed once; then he skidded as he started, roared across the open field, and finally disappeared into the trees behind my car.

I went over to Ben Larch, but remained standing.

"Are you able to get up?"

"In a minute." He took a deep breath, wincing as he did.

I left him. The gun was a wreck. I moved some pieces with my toe, but left them and walked to the edge of the field overlooking the ice-packed shoreline. I realized now that I could see the feathers of a lifeless wing flutter in the wind that moved the weeds around me and the seared oak leaves overhead. I could see how empty the land and the people on it were.

Ben lay on the ground still, more defeated in spirit than body, I thought.

"Come on, I'd better get you to a doctor."

"No." He shook his head. "I'm all right." He rolled over and stood up. When he saw the gun he walked over and picked up the two largest pieces. He worked his mouth until saliva formed, then spit on the tree.

"Can you give me a ride home?"

"I think so." I was still holding my arm.

"This gun was my father's. A Garcia-Beretta that cost over

three thousand dollars. It's worth . . . it was worth a lot more now. I want these pieces."

I had no cause for objection, so I said nothing, but started across the field to my car, running over in my mind the last few minutes. Like most violence, physical or verbal, it happened so fast as to be incomprehensible, or to have only superficial meaning.

That Bob had hoped for a fight was clear, but that he'd gotten more than he bargained for seemed equally clear. The ferocity of his anger had been more than he could deal with, so he had run from a situation that was out of his control. But it had never been his to control. He had hoped to shock Ben with the information that Stedman was alive, and when he had not, he had to force the matter, something he hadn't counted on. Had he meant to hit us? Possibly. He hated Ben, and hadn't swing when I stepped forward. He would have liked to hit Ben, but probably didn't care about me. He had now only to flee. To retreat—something the whole family did well. Something no one had come to grips with. Doubtless they would have been surprised to learn they had so much in common. It wasn't planned, certainly nothing to be shared. I might have believed it was the whole pattern of the case in miniature, the violence and retreat into self, except that someone decapitated a body ten years earlier and left it to become a skeleton. A finally unidentifiable shape. A nonperson. Someone's violence was calculated.

I kicked a tuft of grass, dislodging the frozen snow. I was cold. My left hand ached with the cold. When I turned around, Ben was walking behind me. I waited for him to catch up, but he said nothing when he did. When we reached the car he let me drive. Still nothing was said, though the grievance must have been greater now than ever.

Finally, as we started south, I asked, "What are you going to do?"

"What do you mean?"

"Are you going to call the police?"

"No. Why should I?"

"He assaulted you, destroyed your property and stole your car."

"And you." He turned the situation about, so I answered. "Yes. But I don't think he meant to hurt me."

"Hitting me was accidental, too."

"You think so?"

"Why shouldn't I? He was in a frenzy."

"But you and he were just short of blows when I was caught in the middle."

"We've been that way before."

"What about the car? I saw you get pretty upset with your wife over it."

"I wasn't very angry then." He pleaded defensively.

"And now?"

He lighted a cigarette, inhaled and started to cough. He put it out with his left hand while his right arm shielded his lower rib cage.

"I wouldn't be surprised if Bob's home already. There's nowhere else to go." He looked blankly, past me.

"He disappeared for a couple of days earlier in the week and no one cared or knew where he'd gone."

"He won't do that again. I'll try to make up with him." He made no effort to convince me.

"What about your wife?"

"Leslie will be back."

"You sound awfully sure of yourself. Has she left before?"

He looked at me to gather any intention. "No, but she's talked about it. She'll be back, if only for her dogs."

I didn't think she'd be back. She probably hadn't told him she was leaving this time just to be certain she wouldn't be stopped.

"You expect everyone to come back. Does that include Paul Stedman?"

He hesitated. "I don't know. He hasn't any ties here."

"What about his son?"

"He hasn't cared for Bob for ten years."

"But now he knows Bob is looking for him."

"Perhaps."

It turned out he was right about Bob. The MG was back in the driveway, like the dead gull on the ice, a spot of red against the house.

"You were right. I wish I could be so certain about life."

He gave a slight chuckle as he exhaled. "My family is a good example of the uncertainty in life."

"I was talking about you."

"I'm not any different. On the contrary, I may represent an anachronism for our family. I try to hold on to the past—my family's past, but Leslie and Bob don't care."

"The gun and the car?"

"Yes."

"So you see yourself as a failing traditionalist."

"Not in those words." He gave a friendly smile that was a picture of a man failing, but hoping, expecting.

"Like your mother, with the books and art."

"The car and gun were my father's, too." His voice quavered. "He was a man of many talents and interests."

"Too bad more of us aren't so gifted."

"Yes, it is. Anyway, I'm not at all certain about life. But I'm not without purpose."

"What's that, if you don't mind?"

He looked incredulous for a moment. "Why, my family. The Larch name." He stared at me and finally opened the car door. "I hope you understand that I'm too tired to ask you in. Thanks for the ride home."

"That's all right. I hope things work out between you and Bob."

Instead of going into his mother's house, he walked through the garage court toward his hillside house. He held the gun, one piece in each hand.

17

Bob could have come home for only one reason—to wait for his father. Either he had heard from him already, which accounted for his certainty, or he hoped to hear from him. Both were possible. Since Stedman provided the only possible source of information, his appearance was all I could wish for, too.

When Ben had disappeared from sight, I went to the door. Bob came out as I climbed the steps.

"I'm sorry. Are you all right?"

"I've been better, but I'll survive."

"I didn't mean to hit either of you. When he said those things I went wild."

"Both of you were pretty cruel."

"What I said about Mother?"

"Yes. You know she's not against you. She simply has a hard time accepting what has happened."

"How could he kill that bird?"

"He said—poor judgment. Lots of people hunt." Killing the bird went against what I believed, but I couldn't deny the possibility of a rash, aggressive act that Ben admitted. "How could you destroy his gun?"

"That's different. It's property, not life."

"There is another difference, too. The gun meant nothing to you. Don't fall into blanket idealism."

He scuffed his toe on the top stone step.

"Have you seen your father?"

"No. Have you?" He wasn't being cute. He really hoped I had.

"No."

"You think I will?"

"I'm not sure the way you are. But it's possible. You may be right."

He smiled broadly. "He'll come. He loves me."

I paused, hoping my voice would betray nothing. "After ten years of separation?"

"That's over. It really is. He knows I want to see him. You saw him and told him about me. He couldn't be so cruel as to ignore that."

I nodded, making a forced smile.

"You don't need to believe that. I have faith now."

"You're the one who needs it."

"What do you mean?" He started to scuff his toe again.

"What you did. And . . . have you forgotten that he may have killed the man who was buried near the road?"

He sighed. "Yes. In what just happened I was able to forget. But I don't believe it."

"Believe what you want, but remember the man you're so sure of is a memory. Maybe he's not even a memory, but a picture." I took the photograph out of my coat pocket and handed it to him.

He looked at me, then took the picture and stared at it. "Does this mean you're finished?"

"No."

"Good."

"Why? Do you want me to stay?"

"I don't know, I just do."

I thought I knew. For now I was his security. Until his father returned. Seeing him today made me know he wouldn't fire me, that he needed someone. Leslie would have been relieved.

"I want to see this through," I said.

"What if he doesn't come?"

"I thought you were the one with confidence."

"It's always a possibility."

"Then I think we should go to the police. I could have done that when he broke my arm, but I thought he would show up again."

"Did you?" He was hopeful and pleased again.

"There are no charges against him, but they might issue a bulletin for him because of the sensation over this skeleton."

"I'm glad you think he'll come."

"I didn't say that. If he gets in touch with you, will you call me?"

"What if he says not to?"

"He may. But you'll have to trust me. I'm not after him for this." I tapped my cast. "I want to settle what's gone on here."

"Okay."

"Good. Keep my card. Tell them who you are. I'll make sure they get in touch with me immediately."

He took the card, putting it in his shirt pocket.

"I'm cold. I'll see you later."

I left him standing at the top of the steps.

He never asked whose skeleton it was, if not his father's. It had to be Roscoe's. I'd decided that when I awoke propped up against a tree. I even thought I had the possible reasons narrowed, and wondered if Carlson had. He and I had little to say to each other, and what there was to say wasn't spoken in pleasure.

The police department, like all the other city departments of Green Hills, was housed in a single building, a bastardized Williamsburg affair still decorated for Christmas. Undoubtedly at its construction a decade before, the townspeople were pleased with their suburban restoration of colonial America. All the garages, visible from the parking lot behind, including the fire department, discreetly faced away from the road. Nothing should spoil the appearance.

I found Carlson's office on the second floor. A small cubicle of an inner office, it had a window over the parking lot—where the action was. His frown was unchanged, and might mean a welcome or a preparation for a tongue-lashing when he looked up.

"Where's your candle, Carlson?"

"What do you mean?"

"Your Christmas wreath?"

"Those are for the front."

"Ah, appearance. I understand you want to see me."

"Where the hell have you been?"

"Out of town."

"Where?"

"New York and Massachusetts."

"Vacation?"

"Not at this time of year. I don't ski."

"You seem to enjoy games, though."

"Some. You wanted to play one?"

"I want you to quit playing around."

"Is that all you wanted to know?"

"No. Since you weren't on vacation I want to know what you were doing. And since you don't ski, I'm concerned with how you broke your arm.

"Touché. I didn't suspect you were capable of repartee."

"All cops aren't dumb."

"I never said or thought that." I kept to myself the further specific thoughts I had about him.

"It's a long story," I said, taking off my overcoat. "Let's sit down."

So we sat and I told him that I'd traced Stedman through Ellen Penn, managing to leave out Roscoe and the robbery. Sticking to the bare outline connected with the skeleton turned out to be safe.

In turn he asked why I hadn't told the police about the beating I'd taken. Then he told me how they'd gone through the tedious process of checking missing persons records and connections with the Larches, especially Stedman and Roscoe.

I was forced to admit to myself that if he was holding out as much as I was he'd gotten on the right track without receiving a concussion. We'd each said what we intended to, but we killed a few more minutes making sallies into each other's stories, to no avail. Our relationship would never be good; he had been too high-handed for me to feel cooperative. But because he was closer now than before, he was more pleasant, so we left on amiable terms. Terms as superficial as the building's design.

The only loose end was Marian Larch. I didn't know if she had yet been told that Stedman was alive. Whether she would care seemed more important than whether she knew. By her own admission she hated him. Yet in so many ways she had effectively removed him from her life. Legally she had divorced him and had aided in the disposal of his property. He was dead, if anyone had wished to have him declared so, a step he would not have objected to. More important than the legal distance was the psychological one. She had retreated in time to her first marriage—in name and interests. Ben Larch, his estate and memory were what she lived for. A retreat such as hers was not uncommon, but rarely was it acted out so fully. Even her son Ben had taken it over. He had become the art dealer; she had always been the collector. He acted on a commercial basis for what had been an expensive family pastime. Or expensive collecting can be an obsession. Collecting people can be particularly expensive, for everyone concerned—Paul Stedman, and perhaps Leslie. Once one has collected books, paintings and porcelains to one's pleasure, one must share them or go on collecting, but art objects can cost even more money than people do. The solution is to collect the people to admire them. And what does one do when the people don't admire or cease to admire?

The solution was to let them go and continue in one's fantasy world. Ben Larch didn't believe Leslie would stay away, but he showed no inclination to pursue her. His mother had pursued Stedman before she went back to her earlier life. But more important, she had maintained both worlds at once. She admired her first husband, kept the family collections intact, and performed the acts of noblesse oblige that raised the admiration of Alec Bolen. But she also hated. I could only be struck by the fine balance she maintained between the reality of unfulfilled hatred and the denial of the reality of ten years of her life. I did not yet know which was the stronger in her personality, or which might have influenced the lives of her sons more permanently. They could only go in contrary directions, but possibly for the same reasons.

I saw no purpose in talking with her again. She would learn what happened from either Ben or Bob, and certainly she wasn't going to tell me more than she had already—not for her long-dead second husband. She too would need to wait, the answer perhaps never found.

It was early afternoon when I went to my office, where, if I let myself fantasize, I could imagine the whole thing never happened. If Mary had stepped on the elevator as I got off; if the letter from Chicago had been the only mail. But these didn't happen. Instead there was a phone bill and an ad telling me I could be better informed, more knowledgeable and among the leaders in my community if I subscribed to a new magazine. God knows, I could do without bills and certainly needed to be better informed and more knowledgeable, but I couldn't stand being a leader in my community, so I threw away the ad and left the bill on my desk to pay later. Mary came down when she saw the light, sympathized about my arm, but couldn't tell me any more than she'd already told Chris about Carlson.

I went home, brooding over my dead end all the way.

18

"May I turn the light on, David?"

She pushed the door shut and there was a soft plop as her purse fell onto a chair.

"Go ahead."

I could hear the rustle of the bag in her arm as she crossed the floor in near darkness and turned on the kitchen light. She emptied the bag onto the counter and into the refrigerator.

"Do you have a drink?" she asked, leaning her head through the doorway.

"Yes. Can I get you one?"

"Stay there. I can get my own."

The ice clicked and the liquid splashed. She left the kitchen light on and came in to sit in the chair beside my end of the couch. The light picked up the left side of her face. The darkness outside divided her face, just as it must mine.

"I brought you another Care package."

I smiled slightly at her brightness, thinking how attractive she was in the shadows. "I'm not very good at taking care of myself, am I?"

"Only lately. For which I'm glad."

Neither of us wanted to repeat himself, and there was a slight pause that ended when we both realized we were staring intently at each other.

"I had a very good afternoon." She took a drink. "Your call

has made a difference. Even Howard mentioned that I seemed different, and he never notices anything."

I walked behind her and kissed the top of her head. She touched my left hand, which hung at my side, by reaching across herself with her right. When she moved her hand away I went to the window to stare at the thousands of lights that marked out moments of thousands of lives. Moments— most meaning nothing, but here or there one changing a life in an unknown way. The letdown of events was closing in on me.

"Do you want me to fix dinner? It's late."

"Not yet. What time is it?"

"After seven."

"I saw a family come together today in what I fear may be a prelude to terrible violence. They were better off apart, not caring."

"Not at all?"

"They aren't good for one another. Indirectly they've told me that all along. I read the wrong signs. The fidelities were all in the past, and I didn't accept that when I was told. Or maybe I just missed the separation by accepting the past relations as still possible. I've lived too much with my own life. With you and my family."

"You include me now?" There was a touch of quietness in her whole being as she spoke, as though she were only a voice.

"Yes."

"And what of our need for separate lives?"

"That's what made me miss the point here."

"They seemed similar to us?"

"In a general sense. And to my family. That led me to believe it could be repaired."

"And what of the body?"

"Yes. This family had a literal skeleton. But I suspended judgment. I wasn't certain it was theirs. Not until I knew it had to be Dwight Roscoe's."

"You know?"

"Not for a fact. But I know."

"Didn't they have to be involved, then?"

"Not all of them."

I came back to her chair, touching her shoulder. Then I sat down.

"But now you think they are?"

"Not in murder. But in the emotional destruction of one another. I think only the one who killed may have some idea what he wants, and that's only a possibility. But the others are in chaos because they've only sought for themselves, and when they found no answer they didn't know what to do."

"I don't follow you now. What happened today?"

I told her of the shooting and the fight. The fact that no one had anywhere to go. She listened, her eyes meeting mine in the blue darkness and muted yellow streaks that flowed from the kitchen to the far edge of the couch. There were no sounds outside, only my voice now, and the almost imperceptible fragrance that lingered of her perfume, her presence. It was a different sensory appeal from the ones I had known earlier in the day.

"And you feel your life is tied to these things?" she asked when I finished.

"Not so I can't be free of them, but there they are, in a parallel I can't satisfy."

"An alter ego?"

"Do you think so?"

"Not in a meaningful way. I think you feel sorry for Bob Stedman. You've said so before yourself. And when you described him you referred to his desperation, his insecurity . . . you sympathized with him."

"I do. I think he's fouled up almost beyond relief."

"And is that you?" She let herself smile ever so faintly.

"What do you think?"

"You need to ask, do you?"

I shook my head, as much at myself as in answer to her question. When she had come in she hadn't asked what I was doing sitting in the dark. She never asked, throughout the conversation, what I was thinking. She waited and cared.

"What is the connection?"

"I grew up without a mother; he, without a father. But my

father filled the space. Marian Larch feels sympathy, sometimes, but not much else, and she did nothing for him. Everybody deserves a better break than he's had."

"You sound like a father."

"An older brother."

"No. No rivalry."

I smiled at her observation, then shrugged. "I can't change life for him anyway. Maybe I'm taking that too hard. For a while there I thought I could. Not after today."

"Who else do you feel is an alter ego?"

"Ben, in his sense of superiority. He always feels he has things under control."

"Does he?"

"No. He thinks he does, but at best he only has himself controlled. When his wife left him he wasn't shaken. On the contrary, he felt she would be back. I've had my confidence shaken considerably. I don't think I'm Ben."

"Why not?"

"Probably because he's the killer. He's got feeling enough."

"Such as?"

"He hates his stepfather. Or he did. But the problem is that Stedman is alive. It's hard to accept that he transferred his feeling for one man to another and then killed the second."

"Possible, but you're probably right about such a transferral. What about the mother?"

"Same thing."

"Then you're left with Stedman . . . if you're right about the body."

"Yes. And that leaves me nowhere." I looked at the diluted remains of my drink. "What did you buy for dinner?"

"Hamburger. It's too late and I'm too tired to fix anything else." There was no complaint in her voice, not even tiredness, merely a fact as she knew it.

"I'm glad I went to that party last spring. As I recall, though, it was pretty terrible until I met you."

"Benefits draw out the knowledgeable and the phony. But their main concern is money, and checks can be cashed whether they're written by a phony or not."

"Aren't you serious." I smiled. "Did I ever tell you that ticket was given to me?"

"No." She laughed. "That takes away any right to complain."

"But I wasn't complaining. Am I? That's where I met you. And I've thought about us this afternoon."

"I know."

"Did you? Good."

"I think we've accepted the way we are. I won't change you."

"That's fair enough. You aren't condescending, are you?"

"No. Can I say one thing?"

I nodded.

"Seeing this out is going to make you unhappy. If you feel sorry for Bob, you're only sticking your own emotional life out."

"You're partly right. I don't know how this will end, but if I don't go down the line with him, who will?" I leaned forward toward her. "Besides, I'm not Bob. That's what I said a little while ago. I can come back to you."

"So long as you come back." She leaned forward and we kissed. I had not been so certain of anyone for years, nor could I remember wanting to return as I now did. We moved apart.

"You, too," I said.

19

I slept badly. My left side was sore where I'd fallen. The arm throbbed. At two I took some aspirin and finally dozed. But when the phone rang I picked it up immediately.

"Stuart?"

"Yes. Who is this?"

"My name is Davis. I'm on the Green Hills Police Department. Carlson told me to call you. He's answering a reported homicide on the Larch property."

"Again?"

"On the lake this time." I wondered if Davis was the bald detective who had scratched his head on the pine tree over the grave. "You know where it is?"

"Yes. I was out there today."

There was a pause while his mind went through ordinary suspicion.

"Well, he thinks you ought to go out there now."

"Okay. What time is it?"

"Six-thirty."

"Tell him I'll be there in an hour."

We hung up. I turned on the light and got up. Chris squinted into the light as she watched me.

"Who was that?"

"Someone who works for Carlson."

"What happened?"

"Another murder."

"My God! Who?"

"I don't know."

"Can I get you something to eat while you dress?"

"No, thanks. I'm not hungry now."

"I think I'll go in early." She stretched her arms above the sheet.

"Might as well." I smiled. "We're not going to have any leisure time this morning."

"Do you want to see me again today?"

"Not much independence."

"We don't have many opportunities to be together."

"You know I was kidding."

"You know I am serious."

"Are you going home this morning?"

She nodded her head slightly on the pillow.

"Take my razor and a shirt. I'll go over there to clean up."

"Want me to plan dinner?"

"Don't cook. I'll be there when I can." I got a blazer from the closet. "Anything will go with this."

"I feel as though we're rich. A city place and a country place." She sat up, pulling her knees up to her breasts and holding the sheet.

"And who's the town mouse and who's the country mouse?"

"Why, you're the town mouse. I just have a poor artist's studio. Dave, come here."

I bent over her and we kissed.

"You look terrible." She smiled, then went serious. "You didn't sleep. How's your arm?"

"The whole side aches, but I'm okay."

"It's almost over, isn't it?"

"Yes. I only hope Bob didn't do something foolish."

"Kiss me again." She reached up, letting go of the sheet.

"Can you go back to sleep?"

"No. But I'll wait awhile to get up."

"I'll call you if I'm late."

"So much for your independence."

"Perhaps. As you said, we don't have much time together."
I turned off the light and left.

Traffic wasn't heavy in the gray darkness. Occasional lights twinkled in the morning shroud over suburbia, promising a temporary resurrection. By going sixty-five and taking the turn-off east of the one to the Larches it took me just under an hour to reach the chain that hung across the lane down to the lake. This time a patrol car partially blocked the way, its red light sweeping the area of morning darkness. I didn't recognize the policeman as one of those I'd seen that day by the skeleton. Bannister would be grateful to miss this one. The patrolman had been told to let me through.

As I came out of the woods, I could see a couple of men by an ambulance, two more patrol cars, and two private cars. No one but the two men was in sight. When I got out I could hear voices below the bluff. A light exploded. The photographer at work.

"You get down over there." It was a patrolman standing next to a figure seated in the back of a car. I turned, and when one of the top lights flashed by them I recognized Bob Stedman. His face was blank, unrecognizing, as I walked toward him.

"He's in a bad way," the cop offered.

"Yes." I leaned over and looked at his pale face. "Have you tried to get him to lie down?"

"Yeah. He wouldn't do it. He won't do a thing I tell him." He reached into the car and picked a blanket off the floor.

"Bob. What happened?"

The cop started to talk, then realized what he was doing.

"Bob . . ."

"I came to meet him."

"Who?"

"My father." There was still no crack in his feelings. His face was expressionless.

"When was that?"

"At . . . at five-thirty."

"What happened?"

"I waited by the tree. He didn't come. Then I walked . . . I walked to the edge and I saw this . . . this man lying there. But when I looked he wasn't anything." He was shaking his head now.

I waited until he stopped moving his head, then asked, "Wasn't anything . . . you imagined?"

He started shaking his head.

The cop put the blanket over Bob's knees, coming between us, then touched my shoulder. We walked to the front of the car.

"There is a body"—he pointed in the direction of the lake—"at the bottom of the slope. By the ice." His voice was slow and heavy. "I found it, or at least I found him"—nodding toward Bob—"after he found the body. Shotgun. It ain't pretty. If it is his father, I'm surprised he's still sane. There's not much left to recognize."

"When did you find him?"

"About six. Up on the highway, I saw the chain was down. Sometimes kids break into the property back here. Of course there's no house here."

"It's a good thing you checked it out."

"Yeah . . . I suppose it is."

"You called Carlson?"

"No. That's done at the station. I stayed here with the kid."

He was in his mid-forties, old enough to be Bob's father, probably as good a person to find him as anyone.

"Carlson down there now?"

"Yeah. There's no easy way down, but don't go down just to the left of the tree."

"That where the body is?"

"Yeah. He musta been shot and rolled back down the hill."

I took a wide path to my left. As I started down I looked over to see them putting up ropes to mark off a section of the slope. It was steep and for the most part hard. My feet slipped twice.

"Stuart! Glad you got here so soon." Carlson started toward me before I reached the bottom, even steadying my balance as I skidded the last few feet. It was an unexpected gesture, but no sooner did he have my right hand than he revealed the reason for his friendly manner.

"We've got ourselves a messy situation here. The kid"—he rubbed the side of his nose with his index finger before pointing back up to where I'd left Bob—"says it's his father. I thought since you'd seen Stedman you might make an identification."

I nodded. Sure, I thought, if I know Stedman is dead I can scrap one theory. I started toward the covered figure, but Carlson tugged at my coat sleeve.

"When I said messy I meant that literally."

"It was a shotgun."

"You know?"

"Your man up there told me."

"Oh, yeah. I'm tired. I forgot." He smiled ruefully and tried to shake it off.

"Yeah. I'll look."

He said nothing.

Down the entire slope of the bluff, from meadow to beach where the body lay, a red film was smeared across snow and ice and dirt. Lady Macbeth was right; who'd have thought? Carlson raised the canvas. If the shots hadn't gone to the right he might not have been identifiable. The left side of his chest and head were blown away, leaving only a grotesque pulp. It was Stedman. I was positive enough to say so, and did.

Carlson dropped the cloth, and we walked back up the beach away from the body.

"Thanks again for coming. You must be finished now. Nothing to do but file a high-priced fee."

"Yes," I said slowly, ignoring the dig. "I'm almost through with the Larches. And you."

"Sorry about this. But the sooner we had an identification, the sooner we could tell the family."

"I think the only one who cares is up there."

"The boy? I suppose so."

"You know, he's twenty-one. He's not a kid anymore." My voice was sharp.

"I hadn't thought . . ."

"No. None of us has, not really." I knew I'd viewed him as a kind of kid brother—an adolescent who needed help growing up.

"What do you have left to do?" He was straining to be pleasant, in my debt, yet anxious to be rid of me. Probably sorry to owe me anything.

"I'll take him home. He shouldn't be out here any longer, for physical and mental reasons."

"Need any help?"

"I can get it up there."

I used my right hand for balance on my way up. Our footprints in the snow from the preceding afternoon overlapped the space where the murder had occurred. The marks were clear on the trunk of the oak where the shotgun had been broken. The crushed brown grass and crystals of snow that had melted, frozen to ice and finally been trampled on, might have belonged to a happier time; children might have played here. But they hadn't. Like the processes the snow underwent as it was transformed to broken bits of frozen crystal, the lives of Stedman and his son had gone through stages they could not control. I walked to the edge of the roped-off area. It wasn't difficult to guess that Stedman had been backed to the edge and that two shots had blasted him over, dead before he hit the ground, to roll as his momentum, the only force left to him, carried him. I looked at the ground which the rope told me was special, but saw nothing.

"Can you help me get him into my car?"

"If he'll go."

"Let's go home, Bob."

The cop looked strong enough to have picked Bob up, but he simply led him over to my car, and we left.

"Was he my father?"

There was no point in hesitating. "Yes."

The reply was as painful to give as the question had been to ask. Neither of us said more.

Roscoe, now Stedman. The past could make but one more sacrifice—Ellen Penn, or was her name Stedman, or Walters? The shots that eliminated Stedman narrowed my search to two people, both of whom lived in the past.

When we pulled up to the house there was no visible activity. The cars, except the one Bob had left in the field, were all in their garages. The maid answered the doorbell. She was visibly shocked by Bob's face, her eyes widening. Then she looked over to me, more in doubt than anger.

"He's had an accident. But he'll be all right. Can you get his doctor?"

"Yes, of course." She finally moved aside so we might come in. "The phone's in the kitchen."

"Go on and make the call. I'll get him to his room."

"To the left. It's the second door on the right. In the back of the house."

"Okay."

She disappeared.

"I don't need to lie down."

"You better. You've shown signs of shock."

"Leave me alone."

"Later. Not now."

"I can take care of myself."

"Not right now."

He shook himself to free his left armpit from my grip, but after a token effort he gave up. I took him to his room without further resistance. He collapsed onto the bed, his feet hanging over the side. I swung them up.

His room overlooked the trees, through whose bare branches the small, undulating hills were visible. Below I could see the roof of Ben's house, its shake roof an organized pile of blocks. Had this been one of the lighted windows I'd seen while walking up the hill? An eye on each other.

He was almost asleep when I put a cushion from a chair under his feet and left.

20

Mrs. Larch was waiting at the bottom of the stairs when I came down.

"Charlene told me Bob is sick . . . that he had an accident."

"Yes." She'd heard but hadn't gone up. "Do you want to see him?"

She cupped one hand over the other, holding them to her abdomen. "Is he all right?"

"No physical injury, but he's suffering from shock. Mild, apparently. He'll be okay."

Still she didn't move or ask what had happened. I thought of how, after my mother died, Mrs. Barnes had cared for me while my father spent the whole day at the office. But every night, when he came home, he played with me. I hope I served as a contrast for his long, painful days of forgetting, and I was proof of the life they had once had. Mrs. Larch was unable to reach out to Bob now because she had never tried, and she and Stedman had no life. Bob remained a reminder of insult.

"Was it drugs?" she finally asked.

"No"—I shook my head—"he's not responsible for this. Paul Stedman was just murdered."

"He was murdered!" The knowledge was too slippery to grasp. For several seconds she looked about her without moving, as though placing Stedman in the house they had once shared. Then she turned and walked about the foyer, unable to decide what room to enter.

"So, it's over," she said to the walls. I said nothing. "It's over." She walked back to the study, I followed several feet behind. Leaving the door open, she walked across the room to the book shelves and leaned her head against the books that had belonged to her first husband. The room was what was left to her. Perhaps she was anxious over notoriety, so much more public than Stedman's original desertion. Certainly she needed an emotional intensity that could no longer be created since the object of her hate was dead. That she was sick, and had been all along, was apparent. That she was an object of pity rather than admiration such as Bolen's was equally clear.

After several minutes she became aware not only of me but of where she was. "Do you remember the day I showed you that vase?"

I nodded. "Yes, Mrs. Larch."

She smiled. "My family devoted itself to beautiful objects, to preserving the best from the past, in order to make life more pleasant, more beautiful now. We shall continue to do so. Ben . . . just as his father did. I've decided to donate several objects to museums, and Ben's collection shall go to a library." She wasn't even in the room with me, I felt. Instead she was rehearsing a public announcement, describing her valuables, her past triumphs, her family's generosity.

"Mrs. Larch."

"Yes," she hastily responded before I could ask her.

"Do you want to know what happened to Bob and to Paul Stedman?"

"Why, yes, of course." She threw her hands together.

"Bob found his father's body. He'd been shot with a shotgun, twice, at close range. It wasn't very pleasant. You can understand why Bob is in the condition he is." I could feel myself wanting to describe the whole ugly, vicious consequence of her neglect. But I stopped, let the saliva well up, and swallowed. How distant the vase was, the whole room was, from the little hardware store in Massachusetts, and the scene the previous day by the lake. I'd wanted to find Stedman after he'd smashed my arm, but not this way. Now I could see fully why they had separated—each was too wrapped up in his own desires and interests.

"Who did it?" Her face was completely controlled. "Did Bob?"

"I don't know. But the police will be here this morning."

"Why should they bother Bob? He . . ." Then she blinked, her eyelids fluttered, knowing her question required no answer.

"They will want to question you, too."

"Why? I didn't know Bob went out."

Was she so naive, or only acting? The doorbell rang.

"Just a minute."

By the time we were in the foyer, the maid had opened the door to the doctor, who greeted her formally. He conveyed his self-importance, but tempered it because of his knowledge of his patient's importance. At least he might think that Bob was important in this house. We were introduced, but he felt his superiority and so said little in response to my description of what had happened. Twice I caught his eyes going to Mrs. Larch as though something were catching and she might have symptoms similar to the ones he would see in Bob. He gave up on his spot diagnosis of her. I'd seen enough to be dogged, especially when she again stayed downstairs, letting the maid go up with the doctor.

I walked back to the library. This time she followed me. We stood in the middle of the floor, surrounded by expensive and sound taste. But she had nothing to lean on, either literally or figuratively.

"The police, I was saying, will want to question you."

"But I only knew when you told me."

"They'll want to hear that for themselves." I paused. "After all, it would not take much work to learn that you hated Stedman."

"Have you told them?" She looked suddenly older, for the struggle to put public appearance before her personal responsibility was showing.

"No. But they will come because he was killed on your property, and he was your husband."

"Not now." Then she forced a smile through heavy downward lines from her nose to her chin. "Let them come, though, for I have nothing to hide. I have reason to help, even, haven't I? For Bob, I mean." It was a new idea for her, as her smile flickered out.

"Where were you this morning from five to six?"

"In bed, where I usually am."

"Asleep?"

"Yes, so I didn't hear Bob leave."

"Or come in last night?"

"No."

"How many phones are there?"

"Five in the house. There's another one in the garage."

"All on the same line?"

"Yes."

"Does Charlene answer the phone?"

"Usually. But sometimes we do. I'll take a call in here." The questions had relaxed her. In describing her household routine, she had no fears. There was no smile on her face, however; no expression at all. In fact, her voice had fallen into a monotone recitation. She volunteered nothing.

"Were there any calls for Bob last night?"

"I don't know."

"I'd like to ask Charlene."

"Feel perfectly free to do so."

"Was Ben here last night?"

"He had dinner with me. Bob wasn't at dinner. Then we went over another catalogue in preparation for his trip."

"How was he at dinner?"

"Fine. Why shouldn't he be?"

"He and Bob had a fight yesterday. Bob tried to kill him."

Her eyes widened and she swallowed. "He must not have wanted to worry me."

"Did Ben receive any calls?"

"He made one to Leslie. She wouldn't talk to him."

"Any others?"

"He tried her twice."

"In your hearing?"

"That hardly seems appropriate, does it? He left me in here while he called her."

"And you didn't listen?"

"Never." For the first time she showed fire. She was genuinely indignant.

"How does Ben feel about Leslie?"

"You mean about what she did? Well, it's not your business, but since you've made it clear that you intend to interfere, he was hurt. He still hopes she'll come back."

"Nothing more? Is he doing anything active?"

"What can he do?"

I let that pass, as she possibly intended I should. "Don't you find her departure striking?"

She started to speak, then closed her lips. "What do you mean?" she finally asked.

"That your son's wife should leave here just as Paul Stedman did ten years ago. And during the week the body turned up on your estate, and Paul was murdered."

"Sheer coincidence."

"Probably. At least physically."

"What do you mean?" she repeated.

"Only that someone who is upset might feel there was a greater connection."

"If you mean Ben, I told you he's taking this very well."

"What about you?"

"I was upset. Leslie is a sensible girl—at least I thought so."

"I did, too."

"I didn't realize you knew her so well." Again the indignation, enhanced by scorn.

"We met only a few times." Then I added, "Here," for she needed no cause to alter her already unstable emotions.

"Is there really any reason for you to stay on the case now, Mr. Stuart?"

"Bob is the one who hired me. I think he would want me to find out who killed his father."

"The police can do that very well. And as for Bob, he can

hardly be able to make sound decisions after what you say happened to him." She backed away from me for the first time, turning toward the window overlooking the hillside. I followed, feeling that the pressure of close proximity was necessary, that she might otherwise escape the thoughts I'd forced on her.

"Besides," she began, still not facing me, "I pay the bills for Bob. You've only worked on this case with my sufferance. Now I think it is time for me to stop this, before it does Bob any more harm."

"Is that really your concern—harm to Bob? I don't believe that."

"No?" She turned. Her voice trembled. "You are insulting."

"No, inquisitive."

"Insulting. You imply that I killed Paul, don't you?" She paused. "Paul deserves to be dead. He left me with nothing but a small child. All for some tart, some whore. I am only grateful I had a good family and my standing in the community. No, I didn't kill him, but I'm not sorry. Is that what you wanted to hear? Now leave me and my family alone."

"Perhaps you didn't kill him and he was a lousy human being. I don't know. But I think your son deserves a better deal."

"I can decide that. I can still give him my family."

The word sounded like a cruel and vulgar joke in her mouth. What family, I thought. Only the one that is dead, the answer came back.

"I hope so," I said with no conviction.

"Send me your bill, and please include a statement of all your expenses."

"It's paid. But I'll send you an itemized accounting."

Once again, I thought as I walked down the hall to the foyer, I've found the past standing guard, telling her to assert herself. Well, she had the final say on hiring me. I knew that, and that there'd be no point in arguing over the fact that Bob hired me. He was in bad shape and she controlled the money. On those points I could believe her.

I took my overcoat from the closet but held it over my arm while I looked for Charlene.

She was in the kitchen, cleaning silver. By some sixth sense she knew she shouldn't talk to me, but she did. There had been two calls for Bob last night and she had answered both. At eight-fifteen, before Bob came home, and at eleven. All three members of the family were in the house then. Even though she hadn't had the opportunity to tell Bob of the earlier call, he'd picked up an upstairs extension before she had a chance to get him. There was the opportunity for everyone to listen, for they were all home. Charlene was relieved that I wanted no more information.

Outside, the sky was building up. Layers and shades of gray, from one end to the other. A wind rustled the leaves in the oak trees on the surrounding hill. I wasn't finished yet. I started down the hill to see Ben. About twenty-five yards down the slope I thought I should have put my coat on, to have one good arm to go down on if I fell.

No one answered my knock; I waited several seconds, then cursed myself for not asking Mrs. Larch before she fired me if Ben was home. Okay, I'd try his gallery. Mrs. Larch had paid me for today. I intended to find out as much as I could in the next few hours.

I thought I should call first to see if he'd gone there. Besides, I wanted to call my answering service.

Larch answered the phone himself. "The Gallery." Exclusivity was not only in the name of the store, but his voice.

"This is Stuart. I wondered if I could see you."

"Not this morning. I'm waiting for an important customer." His voice was hushed, as if the customer might have arrived.

"Paul Stedman is dead."

At first he didn't answer. "What do you mean?" he finally asked.

"Just what I said. He's dead."

"But how do you know?"

"I saw his body. This morning, out where you and Bob fought."

"Does Bob know?" His voice was at normal speaking tone, but slow and precise.

"He found the body."

"Oh." Then, "What do you need to see me for?"

Here he had me, so I decided to move ahead without saying I'd been fired. "Some things about Bob and your mother aren't clear."

"What about my mother?"

"I took Bob home. He was in shock, and your mother had a hard time explaining some things."

"What was . . . perhaps I should go home."

"Bob has a doctor and your mother is fine."

"But you said . . ."

"That some things they said weren't clear. They will be okay. Perhaps we could meet for lunch."

"All right."

"Where would be convenient for you?"

"There's a little French restaurant about three blocks from here, Henri's. I can be there by noon."

"That would be fine. Thank you."

I was glad he hadn't pressed for more over the phone.

The answering service said an Ellen Walters had called at eight. They had the motel and number, but when I called it she wasn't in. I thought about calling Roscoe's sister, but decided bad news could wait awhile, until I was certain the skeleton was his. Since the head might never be found, a confession was necessary. Instead, I called Carlson, taking a chance that he might be back. He wasn't, so I left a message about Stedman's wife. Then I went over to Chris's to clean up. She'd taken a shirt and razor over for me, and left a note that she would be back by six. I lay down before changing, thinking how I'd be glad to see her that night, and fell asleep. It was eleven when I woke up. I managed to get downtown in time to keep the appointment.

21

"My mother says she fired you."

"She did."

It was the first thing he said. He held the menu in both hands and did not greet me. We hadn't ordered yet, and he acted as though he might not. But he'd kept the appointment and even taken a table, neither of which he had to do.

"Then why do you continue to intrude on our privacy?"

"You could hardly call your life private. Not with two bodies on your property."

"But this is not your business. The police can handle it."

"Your mother made the same point."

"Again she's right."

"Probably. But let me point out that I have a broken arm to show for my trouble. It's become a personal matter for me."

"The man who attacked you is dead."

"That doesn't satisfy me. I'm interested in why he was so frightened that he attacked me and ran."

"And rightly so." He smiled without pleasure.

I picked up a menu. "Shall we order? It seems we both have a good deal to talk over."

He motioned to the waiter. He had only a salad. But I was feeling better, so I ordered a steak with Sauce Béarnaise. Its substance suited the way I felt events were now coming together. I realized it was Ben's aggressive nature that made me feel as I did.

"Did you make a sale?"

"Eh?" He was preoccupied.

"Your customer . . . this morning."

"Yes . . . yes. A very fine Sèvres ware vase. Are you familiar with porcelain?"

I shook my head. "No, I'm afraid I'm ignorant of antiques in general."

He explained the vase to me, not only the design but the whole process. *Pâte tendres* was made at Sèvres in the mid-eighteenth century, from the reign of Louis XV, in an elegant style. He was very fortunate to have the piece. It was almost as if we had not met to discuss murder. Yet it was all there. The love of the past, of art, or perhaps of the value of art, the sense of control, of both self and facts, and the belief in his own superiority. As he went on about medallions, gold, alkaline glaze, *rose Pompadour*, I thought he might have made it on his own. He lacked the certainty of the buyer, allowing his mother to select the items to be purchased, but he felt for the items as art and he had read and learned what he could about them. I almost felt sorry for him, for the misuse of the past. He had almost made it. But almost wasn't enough.

Certainly what he liked would not interest many, but it was honest, not tawdry, plastic and commercialized. All I could do was tell him so.

"I've been fortunate to have my mother's support."

"Yes. How is it that you built that modern house?"

"Mother said to use the estate, not to buy more property. She offered the lake property at one time, but I turned her down. The value, you know, is bound to go up."

"Didn't your father use it?"

"What gave you that idea?"

"I assumed he went shooting there."

"He did. But that's a long time ago."

"So you could sell the property now."

"Yes. But there is no rush."

"Actually what I was asking about your house had to do with its being modern."

"Oh, that. Ironically, that was for Leslie. We lived with

Mother for a couple of years. But Leslie wanted to take up the offer of land. She wanted to leave my mother's house. I was never really comfortable in all that wood and glass. It seemed unnatural, as though we were going to roll down the hill at any moment."

"I thought a house like that was supposed to seem natural. A part of the woods."

He shrugged. "Perhaps. Anyway, the house was Leslie's idea."

"Are you planning on staying there?"

"I've left it already." He sipped his water. "I tried to get Leslie last night, but she wouldn't talk. I wired her this morning about the dogs. I don't want to keep them."

"No, I can see that."

"What do you mean by that?"

"Only that they don't meet your interests."

He nodded.

The lunch came, an attractive but ordinary tossed salad for him, but a nicely seared rare filet for me, accompanied by the pale yellow, green-flecked sauce. Then I realized I'd skipped breakfast. Between the nap at Chris's and lunch, I'd caught up and felt good. Obviously, Larch wasn't feeling as I was. He picked at his salad, finally laying his fork down.

"You're not hungry."

"No. But that's obvious. Your steak looks good."

"It is."

"But we didn't come here to discuss food"—he paused—"or antiques."

"No." I drank some water.

"Why did you want to see me?"

"Have you thought about Stedman's murder?"

"I haven't had much time."

"Most people make time for something as violent and as close to them."

"I'm . . . Paul wasn't close to me."

"But you have thought about it."

"I told you . . . all right, a little." He tugged at the ends of the napkin in his lap.

"And what did you think?"

"Nothing of consequence."

I shrugged. "Do you want to know what I think?"

"Not really."

"Perhaps you should hear. I think your mother could have killed him."

He leaned back in the chair and, surprisingly, stared me straight in the eyes. "I should be angry with you."

"Why aren't you?"

"Because I'm controlling myself."

"You don't need to, and you know it. Aren't you curious as to why I came to you with this?"

He smiled slightly, finally revealing the upper row of teeth. "Yes."

"Good." I cut another piece of the steak. "Very good. I'm glad you suggested this place. I came to you because I don't want her to be punished. I don't think she's responsible for her actions. I thought you might protect her."

"Do you have any proof?"

"No. My conclusion is based on circumstantial evidence."

"Then there is nothing to worry about."

"Plenty of people are convicted on circumstantial evidence. I think you ought to listen."

He moved his right hand out, indicating that I should proceed, and nodded his head.

"She's been very honest with me about her feelings for Stedman—she hated him, even after ten years. Last night I think she overheard, actually listened in to, Stedman's call to Bob. She then took one of your father's shotguns and kept the appointment early."

"Is that all you have?"

"No. There is no profit behind the murder. No personal gain. No one could gain anything from Stedman's or Roscoe's death. Except in a sick mind that harbored revenge."

"What about Roscoe? Did she kill him?"

"Yes. Both murders are related. For a while I thought Stedman killed Roscoe—to keep him quiet, a personal gain. But he's dead. . . ."

"Aren't you building a thin case? First of all, you assume no one could gain anything from either death. Do you know that to be so? They both probably knew dozens of people."

"Doubtful. First of all, Stedman remained quiet because he didn't want anyone checking up on his past. Roscoe would know more people because of his job. But he lived with a sister and invalid mother."

"You admit his job would make contacts. What about enemies?"

"Possibly. But why was his body found on your estate?"

"You assume it's his body."

"I think we can get a tentative identification from medical records."

"Without a head?"

"From injuries. Size of bones. Foot size." I was generalizing loosely, but hoped he would ignore that.

"You know you haven't given me any proof yet. Only your hunches. You want me to believe my mother killed two men, decapitating one, on the evidence of a phone call and the chance that they were found on her property."

"I said these were actions of a sick mind. Cutting a head off is sick."

"That is a circular argument. She cut off his head, so she's sick. She's sick so she cut off his head—after killing him."

"There's more. These murders sought to destroy the identity of the victims. No head, and a face so badly damaged as to be all but unrecognizable. If a shot hadn't missed partially, he would have been unidentifiable."

"But that could be chance, and totally unrelated."

"Hatred is a consuming thing. She removed them. Not only from life but from ever existing as individuals."

"Even if there is some truth in your theory about identity, how is there any conceivable way of tying it to my mother?"

"You know how she hated Stedman, how she lives for what is past, your father and her own family. She had the reason and the opportunity to kill him. Remember the last point. He died on your property while waiting to meet Bob. Someone in your house knew he would be there."

"What about Bob, or me?" He tapped the tabletop with his fingertips. "Or maybe someone followed him? Some punk hoodlum. You're reaching."

"I know that. But I trust the combination of material I've put together."

"There's still one thing you haven't mentioned. Why did she wait ten years to kill Stedman?"

"A combination of causes. Some may be wrong, but I've tried to figure the various possibilities as carefully as possible."

"How humble of you to admit you may be wrong about something."

I smiled back at him.

"It starts with Roscoe. He was hired to find Stedman and did."

"You think."

"I know. Stedman told me."

"I see."

"I think Roscoe refused to tell your mother where Stedman was. I don't know why—money, sympathy perhaps. Enraged still by Stedman's desertion, she killed Roscoe for his refusal."

"How? With a guillotine?"

"Probably shot him. We know the bullet went through him, since it wasn't with the body, and I think the murderer knew it at the time and so decapitated him to remove identity. Possibly the flesh of the fingers was removed too."

"You have a love of the macabre."

"No. It's nauseating. I take as little of that as I have to. Fear was working too, not just rage, so she came up with the possibility of either blaming or forcing Stedman into the open."

"Through the letter Bob received?"

"Yes. Certainly the letters implicate Stedman. Even without his signature."

"But why wait ten years?"

"Once the body was unidentifiable, it was safer to wait. Fear again. Roscoe hadn't told where Stedman was, and if he had an explanation for his time, the covering of the murder would be useless. To wait and see may have seemed better, too. One murder was enough to hide. If feelings changed, disappeared over ten years, then forget Stedman. If not, he could be killed if he were flushed from hiding. Or I have another theory. Punish Bob. Let him come of age in a way he could never forget. Let him suffer as she has. Perhaps she hates him more than I dreamed possible. At her house this morning she refused to see Bob. She must still feel about Stedman and Bob as she did ten years ago. What struck me originally about your mother was her controlled hatred. I can believe she lived patiently with it for ten years—resenting every moment, but determined to stand it. She's a very strong woman."

"Yes, she is. Why couldn't she be as strong as you say, only more so, and never give in to a desire to kill?" His voice was soft, almost hushed, and even.

"She is remarkable."

"Yes." He paused. "You know you have left me unconvinced."

"I thought I might. You're devoted to her. I hoped you would be devoted enough to help me clear this up with her."

"How?"

"Go with me to see her . . . to bring up these very points. I think it would be a relief to have it in the open. One who kills from such mixed feelings can often be grateful to be relieved of the truth."

"Purging?"

"Yes."

His hand went to his chin, and his expression became doubtful.

"What will it prove if she says no? That she is innocent, or stronger than you thought?"

"That she's innocent."

"What then?"

"By then the day will be over, and since I'm fired, I'll have to go."

He nodded.

"Why should I help you? To hurt her?"

"To know what happened."

"But I tell you I know she couldn't kill."

"Do it with me and not the police. You can't throw out a

warrant. If you believe she is guilty after we talk to her, there will still be time to get a psychiatrist and lawyer to help protect her. That way you can be ready for the police."

"I don't like it, but I think you should know she's innocent. I have to go back to the gallery for a while. Can I meet you at home at four?"

"That's fine. I'll be there a few minutes later to be certain you've arrived."

22

The red MG blocked the road, its right front wheel in a ditch, the left rear reaching for the opposite side of the road; the wet, heavy snowflakes collected on it. Only on the hood did they bead like sweat, then run off onto fenders, down a valley to the running board. I got out of the car and, seeing I couldn't get around, leaned through the open door and turned off my engine. Ten feet from my right headlight was the tree Leslie had scraped as she slid off the road.

I reached over, unlocked the glove compartment and took out my gun. I put it in my belt after I stood up. From the edge of the trees, rapidly falling snow blotted out the house. Fifteen feet up the hill I heard the crack. Knocking me backwards, spinning on my left side, the impact flung me down. I rolled by the force of the blow into the left-hand ditch.

I lay in the shallow trench, a little more than a foot deep, my head downhill. The snow melted on my face, and my left shoulder burned. The deep breath I took came hard. With my right hand I reached for the gun, which had stayed in my belt, took it and reached across to my left shoulder. A small smear of blood stuck to my fingertips. Rolling over, I crouched on my right arm and turned around to face the hillside from which the shot had come. The spot of blood on the snow indicated that the exit wound was more serious. To hell with contemplating the extent of the wound. If I didn't want a hollow victory, I had to think of what Larch would do now.

It was grim satisfaction to think I had been right about him. But to have walked straight into his plan was as stupid as it was necessary. I had thought he would try to kill me as he had Stedman and Roscoe, straight on. He surprised me again, for he probably had known at lunch that I described him and not his mother, whose self-conscious control of her hatred had convinced me she hadn't murdered.

What would he do next—wait for me to move, close in? Not move back. I had to move, make my own terms. The house was still just a shape through the snow. About halfway up the slope the trees were clearly visible. Somewhere between the ditch and there he was waiting, or had been. I couldn't go up the field, but to reach the woods I had to cross the road. I stopped breathing, stopped the hissing tremor that passed between my teeth. Nothing; no sound. The snow made no sound, not even in the trees, through which no wind passed. A heavy snow muffled sound. It helped him and would have to help me.

There was no sure way to distract him, to cover myself. He had to have seen me move, but must have wanted a clear shot. If I fired my gun I might frighten him, losing any sure chance. But nothing was sure. Still I decided not to shoot. Instead I crept backwards on my stomach, pushing with my right arm, until I reached the trees at the foot of the hill, my left arm and side fighting me all the way. I crossed the road in the cover of the trees. To my right were some rolling ridges, spokes from the hub at the crest where the house was. If I worked my way up behind these I might move closer and see him.

From behind the second ridge, when I was nearly a third of the way up the hill, I saw him, moving down the hill, a rifle in his hands. I picked up a dried branch from the snow and cracked it against a tree. He turned and moved behind a tree. Now he knew I was behind him, and I could hope he would look for my tracks in the snow. We both waited, time on his side as I bled. After two or three minutes he moved toward the base of the ridge. Soon he would find my tracks.

I followed the ridge, staying out of his line of vision. When I was far enough up the hill, I crossed down the gully and up to a third ridge and a cluster of three oaks whose trunks had grafted themselves, for the first fifteen feet above the ground, into a single trunk four feet in diameter. This was the place. I went down the far side leaving a set of tracks he could follow. After I had gone about thirty yards, I turned behind some bracken that obscured my footprints and came back up the hill to hide behind the tree. If what I did worked, his eyes would follow my prints past the oak where I waited.

He had to know I was waiting, but he had no choice but to hunt me. I now had the advantage. My coat was snow covered except for the red spot. The waiting was hard, because I could only think, and all I could think of was what was happening, or how my left shoulder would heal. Nothing could control my fearful thoughts. Then his steps, and I realized the snow had made noise. I had made the same noise, a sound that now seemed as loud as the report of a gun. With each step the report became louder. Then he came around the tree and it stopped. The sound in my head ceased when he stood motionless beside me. As the barrel of the rifle passed me, I stood and held my revolver to a vein in his temple. His face was blank—neither anger nor surprise, only wide eyes that had stared into the snow trying to find me. For a fraction of a second I wanted to shoot him; my whole left side demanded that I shoot. Or that I strike him across the throat with the revolver to punish him for my injuries. But I only held the barrel against the depression of his temple.

"Take your finger off the trigger."

He watched my eyes. I returned the gaze, then stared at his hand.

"Take your finger off the trigger. Now put on the safety. Put the butt on the ground and hold the end of the barrel with the fingertips of your left hand."

"You knew." Then he smiled. "I knew you knew. Why?"

The question forced me to admit to myself the risk I had taken.

"I might as well ask you why you sent the letters to Bolen and waited ten years. Why that patient, deliberate hatred?"

My breath suddenly came hard, hissing in my mouth. But I kept my gun at his head. "Turn around and start down the hill, dragging the gun behind you in your left hand."

"I've been a good son." An earnest voice seeking approval.

I didn't respond.

"I have."

"No, you haven't." I surprised myself—there was no anger in my voice.

He stared at me, not believing I'd denied the only relationship he'd ever known. Finally he turned and started down.

"You know where the police station is?" I asked the back of his head.

He nodded slightly.

"You can drive."